STELLA'S CHRISTMAS WISH

It's six days before Christmas, and a phone call to her London office is about to impact Stella's life in ways she could never have imagined. Her grandmother Alice, far away in the Scottish Borders, has been hurt in a fall. There's only one thing for it: Stella must journey north to help Alice while she convalesces. But when she returns to her little Scottish hometown, her grandmother's health is not her only concern. Relationships which have lain dormant for years are rekindled, and fresh opportunities present themselves — if only Stella will dare to take them . . .

Books by Kate Blackadder
Published by Ulverscroft:

THE FAMILY AT FARRSHORE
THE FERRYBOAT
A TIME TO REAP

KATE BLACKADDER

◆

STELLA'S CHRISTMAS WISH

Complete and Unabridged

ULVERSCROFT
Leicester

First published in Great Britain in 2016 by
Black & White Publishing Ltd
Edinburgh

First Large Print Edition
published 2017
by arrangement with
Black & White Publishing Ltd
Edinburgh

The moral right of the author has been asserted

A catalogue record for this book is available
from the British Library.

ISBN 978–1–4448–3476–5

Published by
F. A. Thorpe (Publishing)
Anstey, Leicestershire
Set by Words & Graphics Ltd.
Anstey, Leicestershire
Printed and bound in Great Britain by
T. J. International Ltd., Padstow, Cornwall

This book is printed on acid-free paper

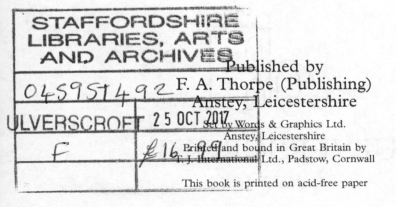

1

The phone rang as Stella sat at her desk in the office, late in the afternoon, six days before Christmas. The number of Alice, her granny, was on the caller display.

Every time she glimpsed the Scottish area code her heart raced. She couldn't help thinking — hoping — that it would be Ross. Stupid of her — why would it be? Not after all these months and their last, acrimonious meeting.

But she'd had her long Sunday call with Alice the night before, they never spoke during working hours, and the quavery tone at the other end of the line sounded nothing like her grandmother's warm voice.

'Stella? Is that you, Stella? This is Lilias.'

Alice's current waif-and-stray artist. Why was she phoning?

Stella stood up and took the phone into the corridor, suddenly afraid that this was going to be a conversation she would not want to have in front of her colleagues. 'Lilias.' She hoped her voice didn't give away her rising panic. 'Is anything wrong?'

'I painted a picture of the house for dear

Alice, because she's been so very kind to me, and we framed it ourselves. Alice wanted to hang it up in the hall so — '

'Please tell me — what's happened?'

'We got the ladder and she wouldn't let me climb up and, oh dear, she only managed to bang the hook in, and I did try to steady the ladder but it wobbled and Alice fell, she fell off.'

Stella leaned against the wall, not wanting to believe what she was hearing. Her mind travelled north to the Scottish Borders town of Melrose, and to the front hall in Hill View, a colourful rug on its flagstone floor. Those hard flagstones. 'Don't cry, Lilias. I can hardly make out what you're saying. When did this happen?'

'Oh, just now, Stella. We had a cup of tea and a piece of my special fruitcake at four o'clock and Alice said, 'let's hang the picture now, Lilias, I want to see it when I come downstairs in the morning'. And now her leg is folded up in a funny way and she won't speak to me.'

'Lilias, listen. You must phone for an ambulance.' It was like speaking to a child.

'I did that, Stella dear. I dialled 999. They're sending one right away. And then I saw your number on Alice's list by the phone and I thought I would ring you too,' Lilias ended triumphantly, as if this were a major achievement.

'Thank goodness for that.' Stella paced up and down. It was something she did when speaking to difficult clients, made her feel in control. 'You've phoned Maddie? And can you tell Gray?'

'Oh yes, of course, I'll phone Gray. His number's right here. He'll sort everything out.' At the mention of Alice's long-time neighbour and friend — and Ross's grandfather — Lilias sounded almost cheerful.

'And Maddie?' Why on earth hadn't Lilias thought to phone Stella's sister first? She was in Edinburgh, a stone's throw from Melrose compared to Stella herself in London.

'But Maddie's away now, isn't she? Don't worry, Stella dear. Gray and I will look after Alice. Don't worry.'

'Maddie's away?' Stella repeated, but Lilias had hung up and the four-hundred-mile distance yawned between them. She hit the contact button and got the engaged tone — Lilias must be phoning Gray now.

How could her sister afford a holiday? Why hadn't she told her about it? And why would she go away so close to Christmas?

Stella looked out over the rooftops of the city, trying to think straight. Darling Alice. Again she thought of the hall floor and those hard, cold flagstones. No good Lilias telling her not to worry. She worried as she scrolled down her contacts list for Maddie's number. She worried as her call went straight to voicemail. And she worried a whole lot more as it struck her that, although Alice had good friends, the only relatives she had in the world were her two granddaughters and if Maddie, for whatever reason, wasn't around, Stella must get home as soon as possible.

★ ★ ★

As she expected, Pete was already in the office the next morning. He looked startled when Stella appeared, pulling her wheeled suitcase.

'Stella! Doing a runner? Thought you weren't off until Christmas Eve?'

'No. Well, yes. I'm sorry but I have to go now. You weren't here yesterday when it all happened. My grandmother's had a accident — she fell off a ladder. I need to go home. I've got a train booked at eight. Is that all right? I came in to show you all the work that needs covered. Look, here's the latest on the buy-out. The main thing is a meeting this afternoon with — '

Her boss pulled out a chair.

'Sit down and hold your horses, girl. Never

4

mind about all that. Think about your gran. In the Borders, isn't she? I keep saying to my wife we should take the kids up to that part of the country. Of course you must go. Tell me what I need to know. I'll get Nathan to handle your meeting — you got the details there? Good. He can look after this until you're back. Maybe you could let the other party know about the temporary change of contact?' As he spoke Pete was rapidly reading the notes on the laptop she'd handed him. 'Is this all? Is this what we pay you enormous amounts of money to do, Stell? Good grief, girl, we won't notice you're gone. You'll be more use in Scotland than idling about down here. I'll sort it out, no worries. Go and make your call.'

He was on the phone when she returned from leaving her message. 'Yeah, now, front of the building. Thanks, mate.' He gestured to her to sit down again. 'Called you a cab. Look, there's this meeting but nothing's likely to happen after that until the New Year, d'you think? Why aren't you flying, by the way? Oh, you don't, do you. Here.' He scribbled on a corner of his desk diary and tore it off. 'That's my personal mobile. Keep me up to speed.'

'But — '

'No buts, Miss Greenlaw.' Pete raised his

thick eyebrows and peered over the top of his horn-rimmed glasses. 'I'm the boss. You've been working darned hard. I've been watching you. If you don't mend your ways you'll be getting promoted very soon.' He looked at his watch. 'Let's be having that case.' He ushered her out of the door and bundled the two of them and her luggage into the lift.

There weren't many bosses around like Pete Parks, thought Stella. He hit the ground running when he came from the firm's Sydney office to take over the department, beginning the same week as her which made a bond between them. Hard work was what Stella needed to distract her at the time and she fell to it, prepared to put in all the hours that were needed. But Pete was interested in getting to know his staff outside of work too and when he found out that she came from the rugby-playing town of Melrose, he included her in the conversation when he bantered with her male colleagues about sport. She couldn't tell him that the game was the last thing she wanted to talk about, so she dredged up what she knew about the town's team, and Scotland's national team.

Except, of course, that her ex-boyfriend had been one of their star players.

'Family's the most important thing in the

world,' Pete said now. 'Never mind this moneymaking lark. It's a game, that's all. Your sister will be there to help, won't she?'

Pete met Maddie that time when she got a last-minute lift down to London and turned up, wearing a white floppy hat with three pink roses on the side, expecting that her sister would be able to drop everything and go out for coffee. Stella was called out of a meeting to see her at reception and of course Pete would have to choose that moment to walk through and Stella had to introduce them.

Crossing her fingers behind her back she said, 'Yes, she will.' Through the glass of the revolving door she could see the taxi waiting. There wasn't time to tell Pete the unexpected news about Maddie, even if she wanted to. A man who thought that family was the most important thing in the world would take a dim view of Stella not knowing the whereabouts of her own sister.

Pete heaved the suitcase into the taxi after her. 'King's Cross and drive carefully, mate,' he called through the driver's window.

The streets were beginning to come alive. Stella watched awnings going up, chairs and tables set out on pavements even though it was a cold December morning, street vendors outside the tube stations, a melting pot of nationalities, glass sky scrapers . . . It was a long, long way from the little Scottish town she'd grown up in. A long way from Alice and Maddie. They weren't part of this new life.

And neither of course was Ross.

★ ★ ★

Stella sat up and rubbed her eyes. She remembered the train pulling out of York; after that she must have fallen asleep. She hoped her mouth hadn't been hanging open but if it had the elderly couple opposite were polite enough not to mention it.

The trolley stopped beside them with a rattle.

'Coffee, no milk,' Stella said.

'Anything to eat?'

'No th — ' Suddenly she realised how hungry she was. 'A cheese and ham sandwich, please.' As well as having no breakfast that morning she'd hardly eaten the night before.

Last evening she'd tried Alice's number again and again but it rang and rang into an apparently empty house. Why hadn't she got her grandmother a voicemail system? But Alice wasn't interested in gadgets and anyway would Lilias have been able to use it? Maddie still hadn't phoned back, despite the urgent messages she'd left. Then she looked up the number for the local hospital. As she waited for someone to answer she imagined a nurse, efficient and sympathetic, picking the phone up at the other end. She would ask the nurse to give Alice her love and say she would be with her as soon as possible. She breathed a sigh of relief just thinking about it.

But the nurse who answered told her there was no one by the name of Mrs Alice Greenlaw in any of the wards. Did that mean that Alice had recovered or — fear clutched at Stella's heart — perhaps she'd been taken up to the Infirmary in Edinburgh. A call there confirmed that Alice had been admitted with concussion and a broken ankle. She hadn't yet come round and the doctors were still assessing her. At this stage there was no need to be alarmed but Stella would be allowed in to see her outside of visiting hours.

She started to phone Gray's house, but broke off when she had the panicky thought that Ross might answer. No reply again from Hill View. Maybe Lilias had gone with Alice in the ambulance.

Her head reeling, she packed a suitcase, hurling in the few Christmas presents she'd bought and the first clothes that came to hand. She made notes on the current state of play with the buy-out she was negotiating, the biggest assignment she'd had so far and now, temporarily, to be Nathan's.

Nathan! As far as work went he'd hear from Pete what he was to do. But they were supposed to be meeting up socially before the Christmas holiday. She sent him a short text telling him where she was going and why, and that she'd contact him in a few days — surely he would understand. It was just as well she hadn't taken him up on his invitation to join him and some of his friends in a rented cottage on the south coast for Christmas.

After a quick slice of toast and peanut butter she fell into bed, dozing fitfully until her alarm rang at 6 a.m.

Now, on the train, the elderly man sitting across from her nudged his wife to look out of the window. 'Berwick-upon-Tweed, dear.'

Berwick-upon-Tweed. In an hour or so they would be in Edinburgh. Stella followed their gaze. The train hugged the north-east coastline and the low winter sun lit the waters of the North Sea. Inland, up to her left as the crow flies, was Melrose.

The train line between Edinburgh and the Borders had reopened since Stella was last home and there was a frequent bus service — but it would still take a good length of time to travel up to the Infirmary every day.

She hadn't thought that she would be in Melrose this Christmas. The plan had been that she would go north on Christmas Eve for three nights, and she and Alice and Maddie would spend Christmas in the new flat Maddie shared in Edinburgh — her flatmates would be away. They'd done that last year in Maddie's old place. It was so good of her granny and her sister to go along with her wish not to see Ross by having Christmas away from home again. Next year she'd have to face it.

Well, that had been the plan, but how she would spend Christmas was the last thing on her mind now.

She'd phoned the hospital again this morning and was told there was no change, which was both good and bad news. Suddenly she longed to share her anxiety with somebody who cared for Alice too. She would bite the bullet and phone Gray.

Just before she and Ross had split up, the restaurant next door to his family's delicatessen came up for sale and he was looking into the feasibility of buying it and running it himself. But as Stella had told Alice she didn't want to know anything about him, and as she headed Maddie off too if she started to talk about him, she had no idea if Ross went ahead and bought it, and if he had, whether he was still living at home or if he'd moved into the flat above the restaurant. She only knew she didn't want to see him or speak to him. Not yet. Inevitably their paths would cross at some point — Melrose was a small town — but her bones turned to jelly at the thought.

She'd caused them to break up and there was no way back — it was far too late to say sorry and she still couldn't explain to him why she'd done what she had.

Her hand shook as she hit the last digit. Who would answer?

No reply. She left a brief message saying she was on her way to Edinburgh.

A long sandy beach came into view. Somewhere out there was the island of Lindisfarne. Once, when they were children, Gray took Maddie and herself and Alice and Ross down here for an outing. They'd driven over the causeway and spent an afternoon exploring the island. It had been gloriously sunny, one of those golden days that stay in your mind. On the way home they'd stopped in Berwick-upon-Tweed to buy fish suppers, sitting to eat them on the harbour wall watched by some inquisitive seagulls.

Now the elderly gentleman was pointing out to his wife that they had crossed the border into Scotland.

Several times Maddie had got the overnight bus to visit Stella, not only because it was cheaper than the train but also, she said, because on the way back she liked to wake up as the bus crossed the border and picked its way in the dawn through sleeping villages. Even though the bus windows were shut, the air, Maddie declared, was different, fresher.

Maddie was the country girl, the one who would help Alice muck out the henhouse, the one who cried all night when the puppies went to new homes. But she hadn't moved very far. Edinburgh was only forty miles away and when Maddie finished art college there she got workshop space in the city and made jewellery. It seemed to Stella a precarious way to make a living.

'Waverley Station. This train terminates here. Please make sure you have all your luggage with you.'

The announcer's voice jolted Stella out of her thoughts. She picked up her shoulder bag and her handbag, took her jacket from the rack, and walked down the train to retrieve her suitcase.

She hadn't been back in Scotland since last Christmas. Maddie was right. It did smell different. Not necessarily better, here in the station, just different. It sounded different too. Funny how one's ear became attuned to the sounds of another place.

And it was different in temperature — a

chill wind whirled around her as she walked out of the station and along Waverley Bridge. She stopped for a moment to look around, at the heart of the city she'd spent her student years in, and her working life before she went to London.

There was Edinburgh Castle, on its rock above Scotland's capital city, imposing its presence on the place as it had done for the last seven hundred years. It was up there, on the castle ramparts, that Ross first told her that he loved her. She averted her eyes, quailing at the thought that everywhere in the city there would be a reminder of him — they'd had so many good times here.

Considering how unfestive she was feeling, the very evident signs of the Christmas season came as a shock. On the Mound stood the tall spruce tree — one was donated to the city every year by the people of Norway, Stella remembered. Beside the dour grey towering Scott Monument a colourful fairground ride whirled incongruously and, further along, a gigantic wheel lifted customers above the rooftops. Silvery-white lights were wound round the trees along the edge of Princes Street Gardens, and on the other side of the street party dresses and gifts filled the shop windows.

The clock on the Balmoral Hotel showed

half past twelve. She was about to hail the nearest taxi when she heard someone saying her name.

'It's Stella, isn't it? Maddie's sister?'

The friendly face, framed by shiny brown hair, did look familiar but Stella couldn't think where she'd seen her before.

'Isabel. I share a flat with Maddie.'

Of course. Maddie's new flatmates were Isabel, who she knew from art college and whom Stella had met briefly once, and Skye who had the workshop next to her.

'Isabel, of course. Do you work near here?' Stella tried to gather her thoughts.

Isabel indicated the large department store across the road behind them. 'I'm a buyer in the homeware department,' she laughed. 'So much for the art history degree. I've taken a half day's holiday to do some Christmas shopping — didn't expect to see you! Have you got off the train?'

Stella nodded. 'My — our granny's ill. She had a fall.'

'I'm really sorry to hear that. That will be a shock for Maddie when she's so far away,' Isabel said, her face concerned.

'Where is Maddie?' Stella found herself reaching out and gripping Isabel's sleeve. 'How can I get hold of her?'

Isabel looked very surprised. 'Didn't she

tell you? She went to Australia on Sunday. There was a stopover somewhere but she'll have arrived by now.'

'Australia!'

'Yes, it all happened very quickly. I never know what Maddie's going to do next but this was sudden even for her! Ross and Skye took her to the airport.'

'Ross and Skye?' Once again Stella echoed Isabel's words.

'Ross Drummond, you know, from . . . yes, of course you know him, sorry.' Isabel looked embarrassed. 'Skye's our other flatmate — Maddie only got to know her this year so you've probably not met her. But what about your granny? You call her Alice, don't you? Is she in hospital?'

Stella burst into tears. Isabel drew her to the side of the pavement out of the way of people rushing to and from the station.

'She fell off a ladder,' Stella hiccupped. 'I'm on my way to see her. They don't know yet if there's any brain damage.' She wiped her face almost angrily. 'But I don't understand about Maddie. Why — was it something to do with her work?' Although she couldn't imagine that was likely. 'Will she be back for Christmas?' But that was hardly likely either — the twenty-fifth was less than a week away. And how come 'Ross and Skye'

16

were involved, she wondered, but not aloud. 'I spoke to her a few days ago — she never said anything about Australia. She did sound happy, quite excited I suppose, now I come to think of it, but that's Maddie, isn't it, and she's always loved Christmas. I thought that was why.'

'Look,' Isabel said kindly, 'it sounds like you have a lot to cope with. Would you like to come back with me for a minute? I'm the store's first-aider. We have a room where we can take customers if they need to sit down.'

'But you've got the afternoon off. Honestly, I'll be fine.'

'It's no problem, come on.'

'It's really nice of you.' Stella followed Isabel across Princes Street and through the ground floor of the department store. 'Alice used to bring Maddie and me here to visit Santa's grotto,' she told Isabel, trying not to cry again at the memory of that Christmas treat with their adored granny. She could picture them now. One year, when they were around eight and five, they had homemade velvet coats — hers was green and Maddie's red — and Alice wore one of her favourite flamboyant hats.

'He's still popular,' laughed Isabel. She led the way up to the fourth floor. 'Come in here, Stella. There's a washroom through there and

17

I'll get you a drink — tea, coffee?'

Stella splashed her face with water. It wouldn't do to show Alice that she'd been crying. Alice. Not long after they'd gone to live with her, she and Maddie had heard someone calling Alice by her first name and one of them, Stella wasn't sure now which, had taken the notion to use it. Now it came naturally to them but sometimes other people thought it strange.

They were a team: Alice, Stella and Maddie. Just the three of them since the girls' father, Alice's son, and his wife died in a plane crash when their daughters were very small. Alice, Stella and Maddie. Now Alice was suffering from concussion, Maddie was apparently on the other side of the globe. And then there was one . . .

Back in the other room Isabel put a steaming mug of coffee on the table and sat down beside her.

'Unless you've got other plans, if I give you my keys maybe you'd like to go to the flat?' she said. 'And we have a spare set there I can give you. Maddie's room's free of course. Make it your base — you were going to be in the flat for Christmas anyway.'

'That's absolutely brilliant, thanks.' Now she could avoid going to Melrose, at least until Alice got out of hospital. 'Isabel, I must get hold of Maddie. Do you know anything about where exactly she's gone and why she didn't tell me? Has she got a new boyfriend or what?'

Before the other girl could reply Stella's phone rang, and she quickly answered it.

'Stella, is that you?' She hadn't spoken to Bette, Gray's daughter and Ross's mother, in fifteen months but there was no mistaking those crisp tones. 'A bad business about Alice, my dear. How is she? Have you seen her yet?'

'She has concussion and a broken ankle. I've just arrived in Edinburgh. I'm going to the hospital now.'

Bette made a distressed noise. 'It was so vexing. Lilias phoned and managed to leave a message. We were both out or of course one of us would have gone with Alice in the ambulance. And Lilias couldn't go because of Patch and the hens, there was no saying how long she would be, and how would she have got back? Although, I'm sorry to say, she probably wouldn't have been much help anyway. She was in pieces when we went down to see her later. She told us she'd spoken to you, at least she had the sense to do that.' Bette paused briefly. 'Now then, after the hospital, you're coming down here?'

Stella looked at Isabel. 'Actually, I'm

staying in Maddie's room. She's away and — '

'Yes, I know. But, nonsense, you must come down here to us tonight. Unless of course you're needed at the Infirmary.' Stella opened her mouth and shut it again as Bette went on, 'Let me check I've got Maddie's address — Abbeyhill Road, number thirty-nine? Right. Gray's meeting friends in Edinburgh today as it happens. Shall he pick you up about seven?'

Bette appeared to have it all arranged. How could she even suggest it? That Stella sit down to dinner with Ross's mother and grandfather, maybe even with Ross himself, as if nothing had happened? Absolutely not. 'But . . .'

'No buts.' The firm voice that kept various local committees in order was impossible to argue with, especially feeling the way Stella did now.

She gave in. 'I'm looking forward to seeing Gray, and yourself of course, Bette,' she said. She raised her eyebrows at Isabel as she terminated the call. 'Looks like I'm heading for Melrose for the night. I'm being picked up from your flat — unless of course there's any reason for me to stay at the hospital.' Don't start crying again, she instructed herself.

20

Isabel handed her a set of keys. 'Here you are. That's the outside door, and that's the Yale for the flat. I'll be back about five-thirty.'

'Thanks.' Stella put the keys in her bag. She lifted the coffee mug and then put it down again. She didn't want to wait a moment longer to be on her way to see Alice. 'I must go now, Isabel. I'll see you later.'

★   ★   ★

As the doorbell jangled forcefully Ross Drummond looked up from behind the deli counter.

'Hi, Mum.' He smiled at Bette, then turned his attention back to his customer who proceeded to take an age to deliberate over several varieties of olives and then wanted advice over what dessert wine to serve with Christmas pudding.

Out of the corner of his eye, he could see his mother prowling around, picking things up and putting them down, obviously bursting to tell him something.

At last the customer left with his purchases.

'Everything all right, Mum?' he asked Bette.

'It's about Alice,' Bette began.

'What's the news? Not bad, I hope.' Ross was very fond of Alice. She'd always been so nice to him — her house was like a second home ever since he and his mother had moved to Melrose when he was nine. Until a year last September of course. He'd gone to Hill View, stood at the front door, and asked Alice outright if she knew what had gone wrong between himself and Stella, what had made Stella decide so abruptly to take the job in London.

Alice had got very upset. She said she was sorry — as if it were her fault — and twisted her hands round and round together, her eyes filled with tears; he'd backed off down the path muttering that he'd try and sort it out.

But he had no intention of doing that. He'd spent a sleepless night after Stella had told him she was leaving, and in the cold light of day he'd texted her, wanting to believe that there had been some horrendous champagne-fuelled misunderstanding, that they weren't splitting up. She said she'd meet him at the café beside the abbey but for ten minutes she'd sat there, virtually mute. It was hopeless.

Let Stella get in touch with him if she wanted to. He wasn't going to try again. The physical pain he'd felt when he'd broken his shoulder in the rugby scrum was insignificant compared with the blow she'd inflicted on him by breaking off their relationship.

Since then he'd tried to see as little of Alice as possible.

'She is still unconscious and she has a broken ankle.' Bette put down the jar of cherries she was holding. 'Ross, I spoke to Stella half an hour ago. She's in Edinburgh.'

★　★　★

Ross turned round and arranged the contents of a shelf unnecessarily, trying to take in the news that his ex-girlfriend, the woman he'd thought he'd be with forever, was suddenly so close by. Of course she would come straight up from London when she heard the news but he should have anticipated that his mother would get involved.

'Ross?'

He struggled to think kindly of Stella, to imagine how she would be feeling. 'It must have been a big shock for her to hear about the accident. She'll be frantic with worry about Alice, I expect. Especially with Maddie not here to share it all with her.'

'Yes, of course. But Ross — your grandfather's keen that Stella comes down here tonight. We haven't seen her for . . . well, you know how long. Dad's known her since she was a very little girl, almost all her life, remember, before you and I came here. He wants to see her. He took the car today so that he could pick her up from Maddie's flat.'

'Down here? Where? Hill View?'

'No, Dad suggested she come to us tonight. Obviously she'll want to be with Alice as much as possible so she'll base herself in Edinburgh.'

Ross waited, aware that his mother hadn't finished all she came to say, and he had his answer ready.

'Will you come round to the house tonight to see her, when you're finished up here?'

That was the question he was expecting. 'Nope. I will not.'

'You can't avoid her forever.'

'Maybe not. But I'll put off the moment for as long as possible. Anyway, it's a very busy evening. We're having the tasting event tonight, remember?'

His mother clapped her hands to her face. 'I'd forgotten, what with the news about Alice and now with Stella coming. Will you manage? I said I'd help but obviously I won't be able to now.'

'The wine merchant is bringing his colleague along with him,' Ross said, 'and I'll see if Tom can spare someone from the kitchen to help tidy up at the end.'

Bette picked up a flyer from the counter. *Christmas food and wine event at the*

Melrose Deli, Prior Street, 20 December, 8 p.m. 'Sorry, darling. It went out of my head. How many are you expecting?'

'About thirty have said they'll come. I'd be happy with that but the more the merrier.'

'It was a great idea of Tom's. He's a treasure.'

Ross nodded, relieved that the conversation had moved away from Stella. 'He certainly is.'

It had been a leap of financial faith to expand the family business and take over the Priorsford Restaurant and its staff, but the steep learning curve involved in running a restaurant had helped him through the first few months after Stella went down to London.

And it had paid off. The incumbent chef was all right but when he left after a couple of months, Tom, the replacement Ross hired, turned out to be in a different league altogether. He used as much local produce as possible and he had the happy knack of cooking traditional dishes with a light modern twist that quickly put the restaurant on the culinary map of the Borders and had people travelling from a distance at the weekends and on special occasions. But more than that, he took an interest in the deli business too and had put Ross in touch with a wine merchant friend, leading to tonight's event.

'What's happening when Tom's away? Have you found another chef yet?'

Ross hesitated, a knot of anxiety curling again in his stomach over the arrangement he'd had to make to get cover for Tom while he went to his niece's wedding — she'd asked him to give her away so of course he had to go. The guy, who'd come when Tom had been on holiday before, and had said he would again on this occasion, had told Ross apologetically last week that he was now unable to. Of course it was a busy time of year for everybody and good chefs were hard to come by anyway, never mind at the last minute.

'I tried everywhere — then I thought of Skye and she's said she'll do it,' he said, trying to sound casual. 'It's too short notice to find anyone else, this week of all weeks, and it's only for one night, well one day, lunch and dinner.'

'Maddie's flatmate Skye?' Bette asked. As if they knew lots of people called Skye. 'The one you — I thought she was a potter.'

'She is now, but she's a trained chef. So after we saw Maddie off at the airport I told her we were in a bit of a fix and asked if she could help. She worked in a couple of good restaurants in Edinburgh before deciding it wasn't for her after all but she's happy to

26

keep her hand in. She'll come down on Thursday so that she can spend time with Tom — see how he likes things done.'

And she was happy, if surprised, to be asked. He hoped he'd made it clear that it would be purely a business arrangement but he wondered if Skye saw it that way. She'd texted him this morning to say she was looking forward to it.

'Well, I expect you know what you're doing. I hope it works out.' Bette reached for the door handle. 'I must go. Last wind farm committee meeting of the year. You sure you won't come round after the tasting?'

'I'm quite sure, Mum.' Ross came over to give her a quick kiss. 'I'll catch up with you tomorrow.'

When Bette had gone, he sat down on the stool behind the counter, feeling shaken. The worry he'd harboured over the last few days — that in asking Skye to come down he was giving her unintended encouragement — receded in the face of this latest news.

Stella on her way down to Melrose! Would she say anything to his mother and grandfather, anything to explain why she'd left? Would she ask after him, even try to see him? He had no idea how he'd react if she did. The last fifteen months, when he'd tried to forget her, melted away and all he could think about was how happy they had been together.

He shook his head as if that would get rid of the memories. That was the past and there was no going back to it.

It would have been unbearable to sleep under the same roof as Stella. Thank goodness he'd moved out from his grandfather's house to live in the flat above the restaurant.

The doorbell jangled again. Ross stood up, trying to appear as if hadn't a care in the world, to greet his two new customers.

And thank goodness, he thought, for hard work. It never let you down.

* * *

Stella got out of her third taxi of the day. She shouldn't have indulged herself, should have got a bus back from the hospital instead. But the stop was nowhere near Maddie's flat, and she was wearing heels and dragging a suitcase as well as carrying bags.

Abbeyhill Road was off the foot of the Royal Mile, near Holyrood Park and the Scottish Parliament building, all of which made it sound as if it should be very grand. In fact, the street looked rather run-down although the steel mountains of scaffolding indicated that improvements were on their way. The stairway up to the flat was clean but the cream paint was chipped and flaking. Still, it was a big improvement on Maddie's previous flat, the one she and Alice had stayed in last Christmas, in a block scheduled for demolition.

Stella hadn't been north since Maddie moved in here with the other two girls earlier in the year so she'd never seen this flat. A burst of colour met her eyes as she stepped into the hall. It was painted jade green; posters and postcards were pinned to a sort of washing-line strung along the wall. A tiny Christmas tree decorated with tartan bows stood on a stool.

Attached to the first door on the left was a familiar ceramic nameplate on which, amid a swirl of pixies and flowers, were the words 'Maddie's Room'.

She pushed open the door and gasped out loud. The room was so, so *Maddie*, that it was hard to believe that she wasn't there, lying on the bed reading a magazine or sitting at the little table sketching jewellery designs.

The woodwork was purple and the walls a pale violet. One was filled with framed monochrome photographs of Victorians, singly or in family groups, captured in studio shots or on picnics or against exotic backgrounds of verandas or alpine peaks — Maddie had always adored old photographs and scoured junk shops for them. Perhaps, Stella thought for the first time, she was pretending that these unknown people were related to her.

Strings of fairy lights encircled the pictures — how pretty they would look when they were lit — and the bed was covered with Indian shawls, sparkly with shards of mirror. Another shawl hung at the window as a makeshift curtain. There was a faint smell of musky-scented candle. A dressing gown, its colour blurred with age, hung behind the door.

Her own bedroom when she was a young teenager in Melrose had posters of horses and her favourite actors, replaced later with some of Alice's paintings. Now, in London, she had neither the time nor the inclination to adorn the little room she slept in. Making the place homier would be a betrayal somehow; it could never be home.

She opened the wardrobe. Along with her choice of wall decoration, all Maddie's clothes were evidently bought second hand too. There was a mixture of decades from which she made up her own very personal style — dresses from the twenties and thirties, nineteen-seventies maxi skirts, a long coat with a fur collar. A collection of evening bags. Scarves and shawls in a rainbow of colours. Everything was old, but clean and fresh. Second hand? Vintage? It depended how you looked at it.

On the floor of the wardrobe was a box of jewellery bits: silver chains, narrow ribbon in various colours, hooks, beads, enamel charms — buttercups, daisies, poppies, shells, yachts, even a tiny striped deck chair and a yellow watering can. A notebook with sketches of necklaces and earrings and bracelets.

On the top shelf was an old-fashioned, quilted-fabric envelope filled with embroidered handkerchiefs. A scarlet beret and a pale gold straw hat with a wide brim. Maddie had inherited Alice's love of headgear, thought Stella, remembering the floppy hat her sister had worn the day she'd turned up at the office. It wasn't here.

She had no idea what else might have been in the wardrobe but wasn't now. December in Australia meant summer, didn't it?

What on earth had taken Maddie there?

She moved to look at the shelf beside the bed.

A framed photograph of herself with Alice and Ross sitting in the dining room in Gray's house, the remains of Christmas dinner on the table. That must have been the year

Maddie got a camera — when she was ten maybe? Ross was still a skinny teenager, tall, but without the build that would later serve him well on the rugby pitch. Stella laid the picture carefully face down so that she wouldn't have to see him, turned it back up rather than hiding Alice, compromised by moving it to the window sill where she wouldn't easily catch sight of it.

A smaller, unframed photo of Maddie and another girl, giggling, heads together, in a photo booth.

Maddie's pay-as-you-go mobile. No signal. Not that Stella had expected there would be. Maddie was always leaving the phone somewhere, or forgetting to charge the battery or top up her credit. And of course it meant she wouldn't have her contacts list.

On the floor was a magazine. Stella flipped through it. She stopped at an article explaining the characteristics of each star sign. She and Maddie were both Gemini, their birthdays close together — herself on the twenty-sixth of May and Maddie on the twenty-fifth, a day apart. When Maddie was little she could never work out why Stella was three years older when her own birthday came first. Even now, when they'd been twenty-six and twenty-three on their last birthdays, she made a joke about it every year.

The whole star sign thing was clearly flaky though. Maddie and herself might look alike with their wavy honey-coloured hair and green eyes but they couldn't be more different in character.

She didn't know what she'd been expecting to find in this room, what she'd been hoping for, but it wasn't there. There were no clues as to why Maddie had gone to Australia.

She threw the magazine on the bed. Out fell a postcard, sent to Maddie in Alice's writing, dated a week ago.

Thank you, darling. So looking forward to hearing about everything. Alice x

Stella sank onto the bed, more bewildered than ever. Hear about what? Maddie cuddling koala bears? Seeing the Sydney Opera House? She put her head in her hands and thought of Alice as she'd seen her this afternoon, in her hospital bed, pale and still, her eyelids flickering as if she were dreaming.

2

Alice is a little girl again, wearing a yellow summer dress and a cardie Gran has knitted for her. The cardie is a horrid shade of green, almost brown, and the wool is thick and itchy. Even at the age of three she knows it spoils the look of the yellow dress, a hardly worn hand-me-down from a neighbour's child, and Alice's very favourite thing to wear. Mam's made her put it on. The weather might turn in the afternoon, she says. Turn into what, Alice wonders. She puts on the cardie and tries not to scratch herself through the sleeves.

But she bounces happily on her toes as Mam does up the buttons because nothing can take away her excitement. It's Mam's birthday and, by good luck, her day off from her job in the munitions factory. Gran's making her a cake. There won't be icing, Gran has warned, nor any candles, but Uncle Frank has somehow managed to buy raisins and candied peel so it will be a real, proper, birthday cake.

She and Mam are going round to the next street, to Gran's house, where Alice goes every day so that Gran can look after her while Mam's working. And today Uncle Frank, Gran's brother, will be there as well. Alice loves Uncle Frank. He can do conjuring tricks and magically find barley sugar and butterscotch sweeties out of the air, some- times from inside her ears!

He makes things too, out of wood. A crib for her rag doll. A tall chair for her to sit on at mealtimes. Little animals and birds to play with.

Alice tells herself, as a secret, that she likes Uncle Frank better than she likes Da. She knows somehow that would be a bad thing to say out loud, so, like the ugliness of the green-brown cardigan, she keeps it to herself.

Mam shows her a photograph of her father every day and tells her that Da is in a place called France, at the war. Alice has never seen him in real life. She was born nine months after he had to go away. In the photograph, Da has his eyes screwed up as if the sun is in them, and he has a little moustache. Alice thinks Da looks scary. When she said that, Mam had laughed and said, no, he was handsome and ever so kind. She only has one photo of him. They'd got married very quietly, Mam told Alice, two days before Da went away to the war. No wedding dress, no guests, no reception, no cake, no photographs.

Sometimes Mam holds out her left hand to show Alice her gold ring.

'We had forty-eight hours together after we married,' she tells her. 'That's all. It feels like a dream sometimes but I've got the ring to prove it, and of course, pet, I have you.'

Round at Gran's, after paste sandwiches and tea and the cake, Uncle Frank finds four acid drops in the pocket of the yellow dress and they have one each. Then he goes over to the kitchen dresser and brings back a box, a flat, black, tin box. When he opens it Alice gasps because inside it isn't black but all the colours of the rainbow. Down one side is a dear little brush.

Uncle Frank fills an eggcup with water and gets out some old newspaper.

'How would you like to have a go at painting?' he asks Alice. 'I reckon you'd be good at it.'

From the moment she holds the brush and dips it first into water, and then into the glorious colour Uncle Frank tells her is called rose madder, Alice adores painting. Gran grumbles a bit about her kitchen table being covered in paper, and about giving a little girl messy paints, but even she is surprised when Alice doesn't slosh them about but holds the brush delicately, moving it in a line with great

36

care, seeing how the strong shade fades to palest pink. Uncle Frank shows her how to clean the brush and she picks another colour, burnt umber this time.

Before they go home she's tried all the colours in the box and desperately wishes she could take it home with her. But Uncle Frank says it will be there for her tomorrow and he'll come round with some nice white paper for her to paint a picture Mam can pin up on the wall.

Alice walks home, holding on to Mam's hand. Inside her head she plans the picture she's going to paint next day.

They're almost at their front door when they see the telegraph boy cycling down the street.

He stops beside them.

3

The front door opened and banged shut. It was five o'clock — Isabel must be back earlier than she'd said.

'Hello,' Stella called out. She went over to the mirror and wiped mascara smudges away before going into the hall.

But the girl standing there wasn't Isabel. She was small and slight with a halo of fair hair — the girl in the photo-booth picture. The girl who'd gone with Ross when he'd driven Maddie to the airport.

'Stella? Isabel texted me to say you'd be here. I'm Skye.' She smiled, in a slightly challenging way, Stella thought. 'How's Alice?'

Stella didn't want to talk about her granny. She resorted to cliché. 'Time will tell. It's early days. You've met her?'

'I've been down to Melrose with Maddie for a weekend a couple of times. Alice is lovely. And the house is amazing. All the paintings and everything.'

She was right about the 'everything'. Alice rarely threw anything out — the house was full of cupboards and nooks and crannies, full of things that 'might be useful one day'. Most of the surfaces were as cluttered as those in a junk shop and you could hardly see the walls for paintings. There was at least one from every artist who'd ever stayed with her as well as her own work. Alice loved planning their arrangement and adjusting it when there was a new one to add — but her days of climbing ladders were over if Stella had anything to do with it.

'Skye.' Stella took a deep breath. Just because Skye had gone to the airport didn't mean there was anything going on between her and Ross. She was Maddie's friend; she'd want to wave her off. But on the other hand why shouldn't she be seeing Ross? He was a free agent as far as Stella knew. A very attractive free agent. But would Maddie have deliberately introduced them — acted as matchmaker? Stella didn't like to think that she would.

It was surreal to think that she was speaking to someone who was possibly Ross's new girlfriend but she had to forget about that for the moment — she needed information. But it also seemed surreal to be asking someone she'd never met before about matters concerning her own family. 'Do you know why Maddie's gone to Australia?' She tried not to sound desperate. 'I didn't think she could afford a big holiday.'

'I expect your granny paid her fare,' Skye said blithely. 'Well, it was her idea, wasn't it? I think she should have arrived by now but of course I haven't heard a cheep. Typical!'

'Alice — why on earth did she want Maddie to go there? It doesn't make any sense.' And where did she find the money, Stella added to herself. The price of the ticket, especially at short notice and at this time of year, would be very expensive, would cost money Alice didn't have.

Skye held out her hands, palms upturned. 'I didn't really understand. It was something to do with an old relative, I think. Maddie was a bit vague about it herself, to be honest.'

An old relative? This was getting curiouser and curiouser.

'She's left her phone, although maybe she couldn't use it there anyway. But I must find out where she is,' Stella persisted. 'She doesn't know that Alice is in hospital.'

'Oh, yeah, of course.' Skye opened her blue eyes wide. 'Well, Ross . . . you know, Ross.' Her voice trailed off for a moment. 'Ross might be able to tell you more. We drove her to the airport and Maddie was talking about it. Although he said afterwards that he couldn't make much sense of what she was saying.'

Afterwards. Stella looked at Skye. What could she say?

As the three of them grew up, their two households seeing each other every day, Ross had been Maddie's friend too. More of a brother really when the three of them were young. It was perfectly natural that even though he was no longer on speaking terms with Stella that he would continue to see Maddie. And get to know her new flatmates.

'We haven't got a sitting room.' Skye broke the slight atmosphere that had developed. 'It's been turned into Isabel's bedroom. Do you want to sit in the kitchen? I'm going back out in a few minutes.' She led the way to the room at the end of the hall. 'Make yourself a drink.' Skye indicated the kettle, and a shelf of mugs, each one lime green and navy but with a different pattern. She shared Maddie's workshop space and made pottery, Stella remembered.

'Thank you. If you hear from Maddie will you let me know?'

' 'Course.' Skye fished in her pocket for her phone. 'Give me your number.' She looked out of the window, at the darkening silhouette of the trees in the back garden. 'It's weird to think of Mads flying into summer, isn't it?'

Stella nodded. 'Thank you,' she said again. She felt like her brain was stuck, clogged with

41

so much to think about that nothing coherent was being transmitted. 'I've left my case in her room but I won't be here when you get back. I'm getting a lift to Melrose tonight.' Now why did she say that? Would the other girl think she was going to meet up with Ross? Well, she wasn't, of course, but that was none of Skye's business.

'I'm going down myself the day after tomorrow for a couple of nights,' Skye said, her eyes meeting Stella's briefly before flicking away. 'Maybe I'll see you if you're still there.' She pushed her phone back in her pocket. 'I must get glammed up,' she said, indicating her dusty jeans and sweatshirt, clearly what she wore for work. 'Christmas drinks party.' She left Stella alone in the kitchen.

Going down for a couple of nights — it was quite clear then that something was going on between them. And the look on Skye's face when she talked about Ross . . . what had her own face given away?

She forced herself to think of something else and went through to Maddie's room. What was she going to do until Gray arrived? She'd put some stuff in her shoulder bag, a change of clothes and toiletries. No need to take the case, not for one night.

With that accomplished she went back to

the kitchen. There was a breakfast bar with three stools under it and a two-seater sofa facing a television. She kicked off her shoes and half-sat, half-lay on the sofa, feeling absolutely shattered. In the last twenty-four hours her carefully controlled life had been turned upside down. Her darling granny was injured in a way that could have very serious consequences; her sister was out of reach in Australia; and it looked as though Ross had moved on in a way that she hadn't quite brought herself to do.

Australia made her think of Pete Parks and work. Something else to worry about. The financial deal she was currently working on was coming to a crucial stage. Pete would have been sympathetic, she was sure, and would tell her to go north whatever the time of year had been, but it was just as well that the Christmas break was coming up. As far as the big buy-out was concerned it meant she'd only miss today's meeting, the one Nathan would attend on her behalf.

Nathan — he should have got in touch by now, to let her know how the meeting went, and to respond to her telling him that the meal they'd planned to have together tomorrow was off. It was a mistake, she thought, to have got involved — well, a little involved — with someone from the office. A mistake to mix business and pleasure.

Skye, in a short black skirt and sparkly top, put her head round the door to say she was leaving and for Stella to make herself at home.

Stella switched on the kettle then slumped back onto the sofa, staring into space, trying to make sense of it all.

An old relative, Skye had said. Something tugged at the edge of her mind. Some old memory. A photograph. Alice with tears in her eyes. But that was years and years ago. Stella couldn't remember who was in the photograph or even if she'd seen it herself but she recalled Alice taking one out from a drawer, and being upset.

The kettle switched itself off and made her jump but she made no effort to get up until she heard the front door buzzer. That would be Isabel. She went into the hall to locate a button to release the outside door, then left the flat door ajar and returned to the kitchen.

'Stella, there you are.' Isabel came in and switched on the light. 'How did you get on? How's Alice? No, don't tell me yet. I'll get us a drink.'

She didn't reach for the kettle but went to the fridge and took out a bottle of white wine and poured some into two glasses. She went back to the fridge and produced some cheese, took a packet of oatcakes out of the cupboard and pulled two of the kitchen stools over to act as tables beside the sofa.

'Did you have any lunch?'

Stella shook her head, enjoying the sensation of the cold wine going down. No, she hadn't eaten anything since the sandwich on the train. Suddenly she felt ravenous and reached for an oatcake. Isabel cut a slice of cheese and handed it to her on the edge of the knife.

'Isle of Mull cheddar,' she said. 'Try it. There's a speciality cheese shop on my way home. I find it hard to walk by; its smells drag me in. Mmm. I'd much rather have this than something sweet. Unless it was one of Maddie's chocolate cakes. Or her lemon drizzle. Skye's the chef but Maddie's the baker in this house.'

Isabel chatted on and Stella was grateful that she wasn't expected to say anything until she was ready.

'Alice is in a room on her own and she looked so ill — her face was like paper and she has a big bruise on the front of her forehead. She still hasn't come round,' she said at last. 'And there was a cage thing under the bedclothes because of her ankle.' She swallowed hard. 'The nurse said hitting her

45

temple would have been a worse-case scenario and that it was normal after a bad bang to the head to be out for a couple of days, but I thought she would know I was there and wake up.' She took a gulp of her wine. 'I wish I hadn't let Bette talk me into going to Melrose.' She looked at her watch. 'Gray's picking me up in an hour or so.'

'Ross's grandfather?' Isabel concentrated on cutting more cheese.

Stella nodded.

'He'll want to see you. I know from Maddie how fond he is of you both.'

Stella nodded again. 'I want to see him. Gray, not Ross, I mean,' she said. 'I've known him since I was five. I miss him. And I'm sure he'll be able to tell me where exactly Maddie's gone and why.' She looked at Isabel. 'Maddie told you that Ross and I were once . . . once an item?'

'Yes, she did. She was upset that you weren't any more. We've seen quite a lot of him here. Maddie asked his advice about selling her jewellery.'

Isabel's face gave nothing away. If there was anything going on between Ross and Skye she wasn't going to gossip about it and Stella wasn't going to, for now, put her in a difficult position by asking.

'Does she make enough to sell?' she asked

in surprise. 'I mean, sell to shops not just herself on stalls?'

'Oh, yes. And it's all gorgeous — she's getting a name for herself. Hopeless on the business side though, which is where Ross comes in. He's helping her with her accounts and he's found someone to make her a website.'

'Good for her.' Stella filed away the information. One more thing to ask Maddie about when they eventually caught up with each other. With Ross being a taboo subject, she hadn't heard about any of that. 'Well, I hope Ross won't be there tonight. I don't think I could cope with seeing him on top of everything else. We didn't exactly part on good terms. But can I come back here, Isabel? I'll pay my way. Of course Alice and I were going to stay here for Christmas anyway but that wasn't until Christmas Eve, and now that Maddie's not . . . '

'Of course you can. Don't talk about paying. Anyway, Maddie's rent is all paid up. Would you like some more?' Isabel poured wine into Stella's glass. 'Just take it a day at a time. The doctors will know more tomorrow and surely Alice will be awake and able to talk.'

'You're right,' Stella said gratefully. 'Thank you, Isabel. For everything. I'm sorry to have landed on you like this when you hardly know me.'

'No need to be. I feel I do know you anyway. Maddie talks a lot about you.'

'Does she? What does she say?' she asked curiously. Her new friends in London — mostly colleagues since she'd made little effort to have a social life outside of work — didn't talk much about their families so she couldn't imagine herself chatting to them about Alice and Maddie.

'Oh, about when you were children. Little things. Dresses you had. Picnics. Puppies and kittens. Scrapes you got her out of. The time when she got lost in the mist and you found her.'

Stella laughingly disclaimed any heroism. 'That sounds much more dramatic than it was. She was only at the end of the garden.'

'It was big sister to the rescue, as far as Maddie's concerned. You're very important to her, you know, if I may say so,' Isabel said. 'She misses you.'

'I miss her, and Alice. It's when you're away from people for a while that you really appreciate them.' No, Stella told herself, she wasn't thinking of Ross but of her sister and grandmother. She would give anything if they could both be with her here right now, in this little kitchen. The three of them would be congregated around the cooker, stirring, tasting, laughing, clattering cutlery down on the table, enjoying a meal together, mock arguing over whose turn it was to wash up . . .

The doorbell rang.

Isabel went to answer the intercom. 'Hello? I'll buzz you in. Oh, right, I'll tell her. That's Gray,' she said, coming back from the hall. 'He's double-parked so he can't come up.'

'I'll see you tomorrow, Isabel.' Stella dashed to the bedroom for her luggage. 'Thank you for the drink and that lovely cheese. Exactly what I needed.'

She hurried downstairs. She was so looking forward to seeing Gray. He'd been part of her life for over twenty years since she and Maddie went to live with Alice. She only hoped that the split between herself and Ross wouldn't make any difference to her relationship with Ross's grandfather.

* * *

Ross turned the sign to read 'Closed' and pulled the blind down. An hour and a half before tonight's event kicked off.

There was a noise at the connecting door that he'd had made between the deli and the restaurant. Tom came through, manoeuvring

49

a couple of trestle tables, his usually florid face even ruddier with the exertion.

'Everything all right in the kitchen?' Ross asked, as the chef helped him set the trestles up and cover them with cloths patterned in Christmassy red and green.

Tom nodded. 'Aye, calm before the storm. Oh, the guy who was going to bring the pheasants today — he phoned to say his van's broken down. He'll get them to us tomorrow. It's not a problem. Your Skye's coming down on Thursday, isn't she? Do a lunch and dinner with me? Then I can tell her what we've in the store and how I like things done.' He rolled his eyes. 'Why did my niece have to get married two days before Christmas? We've got so many bookings — the busiest we've ever been.'

'Don't worry about it,' Ross said. 'It's a big day for you. At least you don't have to travel far and it's just one lunch and one dinner time you'll miss.' It was a concern though, he thought, when so many new customers would be eating in the restaurant, customers he hoped would leave with a favourable impression of the food and tell all their friends, leave good reviews online . . . But he should clear up any misapprehension that Tom might be under. 'Your very temporary deputy chef, mate, by the way, not 'my Skye'.'

earlier, was keeping the conversation light, knowing that her concern about Alice must be overwhelming. And of course he would also be trying not to mention Ross. But she couldn't help laughing at his last remark — natives of Border towns were famous, perhaps even infamous, for being fiercely loyal to their own patch of the country. 'If only!' she said.

Gray seemed relieved to hear her laugh. 'So how are things in the City of London? What are you working on?'

So he was going to act as though she hadn't caused a big upheaval in his grandson's life. As if he hadn't written her a letter saying how sorry he was about the split, that Ross was stomping about like a thundercloud, and excuse him for interfering but was there any chance of a reconciliation? As if she hadn't sent a short note in reply saying she was sorry too, and no, there wasn't.

'The management buy-out of one of the big DIY shops,' she answered, trying to sound offhand. Gray used to help her with her maths homework until she knew more than he did, but he would understand that this was a big deal, a feather in her cap.

'Big stuff, eh?' he whistled. 'Was it difficult to get away?'

'The timing wasn't too bad. I've missed one meeting but it should all go quiet now until after New Year. My boss is great — he was very sympathetic.'

'Good,' said Gray. 'It looks as if it's been a successful move for you then,' he added, his tone cautious, treading delicate ground. 'Alice worries about you, you know.'

'I know she does. I'm fine. It's a nice company. I'm really busy, long hours, but I enjoy it. And I like London.' It was true. The work was intense but satisfying, and now that she'd got more used to the city, London had gone from a noisy blur to being undeniably an exciting place to live.

Gray changed the subject. 'I went to see Lilias last night, see how she was coping. I think she is, just, coping I mean, but she's nervous about being in the house on her own. She'll be glad of your company.'

But it wasn't Lilias that Stella wanted to hear about. 'Gray, Isabel says that Maddie's in Australia. What on earth is she doing there? We'll have to let her know what's happened.'

Gray slowed down as they came to the roundabout at Cameron Toll. 'Did Alice not speak to you about it? She told me she was going to tell you — probably she was planning to phone you last night but of course she couldn't.'

'Tell me what? I had no idea Maddie was anywhere other than in Edinburgh.'

'It's a rather difficult story and not mine to tell.' Gray turned to look at her briefly.

Stella knotted her fingers together in her lap. Her grandmother, her sister, and now Gray, Alice's oldest friend — what were they hiding from her?

'It's something that cropped up completely out of the blue, Stella,' Gray added. 'It's a family thing. Alice will — '

'But you're like family, Gray! Maddie and I have known you forever.'

Gray fumbled to pat Stella's hand, returning his own to the steering wheel as they came to a corner. 'It's something very unexpected but very good, I promise. You should hear it from Alice herself.'

Stella looked out of the window. If Gray knew about whatever it was and thought that it was good, that was a relief, but she was still none the wiser about what on earth could involve Maddie setting off into the wide blue yonder. 'A family thing', Gray had said. And it was about 'an old relative' according to Skye. But Alice didn't have any family, no relatives apart from Maddie and herself . . .

There was a lump in her throat and a thought that made her eyes prickle so she turned further round in her seat in case the prickles turned into tears she didn't want Gray to see. Was it only because Stella was down in London, immersed in her job, that Alice had confided in her younger grand-daughter. Or was there some other reason?

Alice didn't have a favourite; Stella knew that. But in temperament Maddie and Alice were so very alike. Artistic, impulsive. Innocent. It was a strange word to use to describe a woman in her seventies but Alice went through life now as she had always done, her pansy-brown eyes full of confidence in everyone she met, full of the trust that led her to invite artists into her home — whether they were waiting for their big break, having nervous breakdowns or down on their luck in some way — sometimes people she barely knew.

Some of them, even in Alice's opinion, had overstayed their welcome. But the bad experiences never discouraged her from offering hospitality to the next person in need, currently Lilias.

Maddie had the same instincts. She never just gave money to *Big Issue* sellers and moved swiftly on. After she'd bought a copy she stopped to talk to them, hunkered down to pat their dogs. Like Alice she was always late, always losing things, always acting impulsively rather than setting out the pros and cons of a course of action, as Stella would do.

Did Alice and Maddie think that Stella would not approve of the action they were taking over whatever had arisen? That she wouldn't have helped?

As they left the city behind and the dark outline of the Border hills came into view Stella wished she could open the window to let the cold fresh air in, smell her native heath, blow the cobwebs away. They'd certainly get blown away in this wind, she thought, seeing the trees dipping and swaying.

'Home territory now, eh, Stella?'

Gray hated having to drive up to town. In Stella's memory, a quick dash to the cash-and-carry was usually his limit but of course now that Ross had taken over the deli Gray wouldn't have to do that any more. It was good of him to drive through Edinburgh in the rush hour to pick her up but it was typical of the reliable friend who had been there whenever Alice or her granddaughters needed him for as long as Stella could remember.

She nodded, trying to make out familiar landmarks.

'How long is it since you were last up?' Gray's tone was light.

Stella tried to match it. 'Last Christmas. I stayed in Maddie's old flat and Alice came up to Edinburgh and stayed too, remember? Bette kindly asked Lilias for Christmas dinner.' And that was the arrangement in place for this year too.

They'd had fun, the three of them, last Christmas.

Making Christmas dinner in that awful old cooker, eating it off their knees because there wasn't a table. Persuading Alice to go on the big wheel in Princes Street. She'd loved the view from the top so much that they went round again, after which they ate crepes with chocolate sauce in the German market. Alice in Maddie's bed, her granddaughters in sleeping bags on the floor. It was hardly a comfortable arrangement but it was only four months after the break-up with Ross and she couldn't face going to Melrose as if nothing had happened. How good it had been of Alice and Maddie to make an adventure of it.

Gray nodded without comment.

'I talk to Alice every Sunday,' Stella said, trying not to sound defensive. Not that the calls were very satisfactory, for either of them. Stella wanted to hear about what Alice and Maddie were doing but about nothing that involved Ross. And she had to spend a lot of the call reassuring Alice that she wasn't being worked into the ground.

Gray slowed down as he drove over the bridge and Hill View, Alice's home, came into sight, illuminated under the moon. It had its back to the road, though not in an unfriendly way, Stella used to think. It was just that, as its name indicated, it would rather look up to the hills that the Roman soldiers had tramped over so long ago. When they were young she and Ross used to sit out for hours in the summer hoping and hoping that the legendary lost legion would march by.

'Will you be seeing Lilias tomorrow?' Gray returned to the subject of Alice's lodger.

'I'll ring the hospital first thing and I'll pop in on Lilias and tell her what the latest news is,' Stella said. 'And I need to pack a bag for Alice. She doesn't have anything with her, the nurse told me. Not even a toothbrush. I suppose the accident happened so quickly and Lilias was so upset that she didn't think of it.'

'She's a nervy sort of person, easily flustered,' Gray said. 'Have you seen her paintings? They're very good.' That was nice of Gray, bless him. She suspected he was no more a critic of what was good art than she was herself. That gene had passed her by and given Maddie a double helping.

'What? No, I've only met her one or twice.

61

Some friend of Alice's introduced them not long before I went to London.'

'She really doesn't like being in the house on her own. She — '

Stella could see where this conversation was going. She would have to nip it in the bud right now.

'It will be lovely to have the night here with you and Bette,' she said, 'but tomorrow I'm going back to Edinburgh. I can stay in Maddie's room. I must be near Alice. I'll go and see Lilias tomorrow and I'll keep in touch with her but I won't stay.' A thought occurred to her. 'Maybe I could take Alice up some photos and books as well, her own things.'

Gray nodded slowly. 'Sense in that,' he said. 'Well, Lilias will just have to get on with it. Either Bette or I go over in the evening to check all's well. And I've asked . . . I've asked Ross to look in on her in the mornings, see if there are any odd jobs that need doing. And she's got old Patch for company.'

The colour rose in Stella's face at the mention of Ross's name and as they drove down Prior Street her heart hammered as she saw the deli. Although it was after eight o'clock the lights were on and it was full of people. The restaurant was all lit up too and from what she could see it had been painted to match the shop with spruce black paintwork and window boxes. So the plan to buy it must have gone ahead. Altogether, it looked a thriving and successful concern.

'Ross is living above the restaurant now, did you know? There's a small flat up there,' Gray said. 'He won't be joining us this evening.'

Stella felt a huge wave of relief. She'd been psyching herself up to the possibility of seeing him but had no idea how she would react if it actually happened.

Thankfully, Gray didn't seem to want a response as he turned into Priorsford Road. 'Right, my dear, we're here. There's Bette at the window.'

Gray was over six feet tall and Ross topped him by a couple of inches. The woman who was their daughter and mother respectively barely made five feet but what she lacked in height she made up for in personality. She had a finger in most pies in the area, chairing committees and galvanising people into action of various sorts.

But her voice was warm now as she came down the path to greet them. 'Stella, it's so good to see you. We've missed you.' Bette didn't do hugs but she held Stella's arm as she ushered her inside.

The carved chest in the hall still had its

huge bowl on top of it, filled at this time of year with holly and greenery. Underneath were the scents that could conjure up this house for Stella wherever she smelt them — freshly cut logs; the cinnamon candles that Bette burned and the pine essence she liked to use in the bath; something good cooking in the kitchen.

Not everything had stayed the same though. The Victorian fireplace had been replaced with a wood-burning stove. Maybe it was more practical but it wasn't so pretty. Stella's head reeled as she sat down in the old chintz armchair under the soft glow of the shaded wall lights. She'd always loved this room, especially in winter.

The room she had in London wasn't a home, not like this or Hill View, merely a place to lay her head really, owned by a faceless landlord. There were others in the property, each renting their bedrooms individually but sharing the facilities, but they came and went; it wasn't a proper flat share like Maddie's.

She'd had so many happy times in this house. Although it was much tidier and less cluttered than Hill View it was still welcoming and homely. Every Christmas Eve Bette threw a wonderful party for friends and neighbours. The dining-room table was laden with food; a tree covered with candle-shaped lights took up the bay window space. Mistletoe hung above every doorway . . .

On the side-table next to her chair was a photograph of Ross with his father, Kenneth, both laughing. It looked as though it had been taken recently, perhaps the last time Kenneth was home, so it was the first Stella had seen of Ross since she left. Her heart flipped over. It was as if he were smiling at her, laughter lines crinkling up his face beside his dark blue eyes.

'How is Kenneth?' she asked Gray, dragging her eyes away and trying to blot from her mind the thought of that Christmas Eve three years ago when Ross's kiss under the mistletoe and her response to it changed their relationship forever.

'Well, that's our big news,' said Gray. 'He's got fed up working abroad. It's a younger man's game, he says.'

Bette came through from the kitchen, a dishcloth over her arm, and nodded vigorously in agreement. She and Kenneth and nine-year-old Ross had come to live with Gray when his wife died. The house was too big for Gray on his own and, as an engineer, specialising in building power plants in developing countries, Kenneth could be based anywhere. Bette had flung herself back into life in Melrose where she'd grown up and Ross settled quickly into school and into after-school friendship with the Greenlaw sisters.

'He's giving it up,' Gray went on. 'Going into partnership with an old engineering colleague in Glasgow. So we're going to be losing Bette, but it will be great for her and Kenneth to have a home of their own again. When he comes back on Friday it will be for good.'

'Whatever will you do without her?' Gray would miss the company and all the home comforts his daughter provided so well.

'I'm very worried about that,' Bette said. 'I've started to put out some feelers to find him a housekeeper.'

'I don't need a housekeeper,' Gray protested. 'Or want one.'

'We'll go on arguing about that, I daresay,' Bette said. 'Dinner's ready. Come through, Stella. I thought we'd eat in the kitchen. It's cosier than the dining room.'

'It's good to have you here.' Gray clapped Stella on the back as he went to his own place at the table. 'Don't leave it so long the next time.'

He and Bette seemed to have agreed beforehand that if they mentioned Ross — and it would be odd if they didn't — it would only be in passing and no questions were to be asked about anything controversial. So they talked about Alice; about neutral matters of interest; they asked about her job.

So when she finished her chicken wrapped in bacon, potato gratin and sautéed cabbage, Stella put down her knife and fork and appealed directly to Bette.

'Do you know where exactly Maddie's gone and why, Bette? Why is it all such a mystery?'

Bette and her father exchanged glances and Stella thought she saw Gray shake his head imperceptibly.

'I believe she flew to Sydney first,' Bette said, 'then there was another flight I think. As Dad's probably said to you it's a rather complicated family thing and you should really hear about it from Alice. We don't know the whole story or even half of it.' She began to clear the plates. 'I thought we might have heard from Maddie by now, if only to say she arrived safely, but she's such a scatterbrain. She promised Ross that she would buy a mobile — one that works internationally — as soon as she arrived.'

'She may have phoned Alice of course,' Gray said, as Bette disappeared through to the kitchen again.

'No.' Stella looked at him in dismay. 'I

don't want her to hear about the accident from Lilias.'

'You'll see Lilias in the morning,' Gray said, putting his hand over hers. 'But if Lilias hasn't told Maddie I wonder if you should maybe keep the news about Alice from her at this stage, Stella? Or at least tone it down. There's nothing she can do.'

'Oh, I must — ' Stella stopped. No, she realised, Gray was right. There was nothing Maddie could do except be alarmed and upset. But she would ask about Alice obviously and wonder why she couldn't come to the phone. And of course it depended on how well Alice recovered — what report the hospital would have on her tomorrow.

'I can't think straight, Gray.' She put her other hand on top of his for a moment. 'But I feel better for seeing you.'

'You look very tired, my dear.' Bette put a baking dish down on the table. 'Have a little helping of this — it's very light. Then a cup of tea and an early night? You must have been up at the crack of dawn.'

'It feels like weeks since I left London.' Stella looked at her watch. 'But it's only about thirteen hours since I got on the train.' She took a spoonful of warm orange soufflé. 'This is delicious, Bette. I think I've forgotten what home cooking's like. I live on eggs and apples and toast, more or less.'

'You're too thin. You should look after yourself better,' Bette scolded. 'But you must lead an exciting life with your busy job and all that London has to offer. I'd love to hear more about it sometime.'

It sounded as if she meant it but Stella wondered what she really thought. After all, in leaving here, in going south, Stella had hurt Ross badly. It was generous of Ross's mother to apparently not hold that against her. Or maybe it meant that Ross had found someone else whom Bette would be happy to see with her only son. Maybe they had all moved on.

Stella suddenly felt that she couldn't stay awake for another minute and was about to pitch forward embarrassingly into her pudding bowl.

She smiled shakily at Bette. 'I think I'll save the cup of tea for the morning if you don't mind.'

4

A wintry sun was poking yellow fingers through the curtains when Stella woke up. She rolled over and looked at her watch. Nine o'clock!

Alice. She grabbed her phone and called the hospital. No change.

In ten minutes she was washed and dressed and down in the kitchen.

'I should have got up earlier,' she said to Bette. 'I never thought I'd sleep so long.'

'Dad thought you should be left. He sends his love; he had a dentist's appointment this morning,' Better said. 'You needed that rest.'

'Maybe I did,' Stella admitted. She updated Bette on Alice.

'I hope there'll be better news this afternoon,' Bette said sympathetically. 'Now, bacon, cereal, toast?'

'Toast would be lovely, thanks.' Stella wandered over to look out of the window. If you stood at a certain angle you could see the pantiled roof and high chimneys of Alice's house on the other side of the field. The hills above it were dusted with snow.

'Do you know when the next bus leaves?'

'What a good idea, clever girl,' Bette said. She went to a cupboard and produced a tartan holdall. 'Now, you'll phone us with news — of Alice or of Maddie?'

'I will,' promised Stella.

She stepped forward and then stopped, wondering if Bette would want to be embraced. She held out her hand instead and Bette clasped it in both of hers.

'We'll speak soon, Stella. What do you think you'll do about Christmas? You can't spend it on your own in Edinburgh.'

'I've no idea. I hadn't thought about it.' *And I'm not going to think about it now.* 'Give my love to Gray, Bette. I'll be in touch.'

★ ★ ★

When they were children, Stella and Maddie and Ross never visited each other by using the road between the two houses. They ran diagonally across the field at the back and jumped the stepping stones in the burn below Hill View, slipping off them and getting their feet soaked as often as not. But grown-up Stella walked along Priorsford Road and round the corner into Eildon Street.

She would have about fifteen minutes with Lilias and then she could catch the 10.40 bus. It wasn't very long but surely Lilias would understand that she had to be in Edinburgh.

There was smoke rising now from one of the chimneys so Lilias was evidently up and about and capable of lighting that old range in the kitchen. Alice loved it but the intricate arrangement of dampers and flues confounded most other people.

The window frames could do with repainting, as could the garden gate. And some of the distinctive terracotta-coloured tiles were missing, she noticed. How long had it been since that happened and how much would they cost to replace?

She hesitated at the door. Ordinarily of course she would just walk in but that would give Lilias a fright and besides it didn't feel like it was home without Alice. She compromised by knocking loudly, opening the door and calling, 'Hello. Lilias? It's Stella.'

A wispy little figure wearing an old wool dress and cardigan appeared at the end of the corridor.

Behind her came a tall, dark-haired man in jeans and a blue shirt, ducking as he came through the kitchen door.

Ross.

Stella took a step backwards. If only she could keep walking backwards, rewinding herself back to Edinburgh, back to London.

'Come in, Stella. Do come in. Poor dear Alice. I'll never forgive myself. If only I hadn't given her the painting . . . ' Lilias reached Stella and took hold of one of her hands, tugging it gently but insistently. 'Gray's grandson is here. He got that dreadful range going for me. Ross, this is Stella, Alice's granddaughter.'

'Yes, I know.'

Stella lifted her head to meet his eyes. The same deep blue eyes she'd seen in the photograph at Gray's, but today they were as cold as a winter sky. She felt a chill run through her.

'If there's nothing else, Lilias?' Ross tried to get past them.

'Oh, but you must both have a cup of my special herbal tea. I insist. You've worked so hard for me this morning, Ross dear, and Stella dear, we must talk.'

She pulled Stella down the narrow corridor towards the kitchen and Ross had no choice but to retreat in front of them.

'Of course you'll know each other, childhood friends, how silly of me.' Lilias ushered them to the table. 'You must have a lot to catch up on.' She stood beside Stella and clasped her hands. 'Have you seen Alice? Did she speak? Will she live?'

'Of course she'll live,' Stella said sharply. The alternative was not to be contemplated. She softened her tone, seeing how miserable Lilias looked. 'She's still unconscious, Lilias, but she's doing as well as can be expected.' Not that the nurses had actually said that but it was a soothing thing for Lilias to hear. It soothed herself a little too. 'I'll visit her this afternoon and of course if she's come round I'll tell her I was here.'

Like a plant being watered, Lilias visibly cheered up. She took a brown teapot over to the sink and rinsed it under the tap several times, like some sort of ritual.

Stella and Ross sat like statues, one on either side of the table, while their hostess went on to mix together leaves from various packets, all the time making inconsequential remarks. Stella was glad of the fuss and bustle she made, hoping that it disguised the lack of conversation between her guests.

She sneaked a look at Ross's hands, remembering them holding her, touching her. They'd been one of the things she loved best about him. Strong, capable hands. Some dark hair showing beneath his shirt cuffs. Yes. They were still the same. She looked away.

Lilias felt the kettle on the range. 'Not boiling yet. Alice's dear old whistling kettle. I'll get some biscuits.' She disappeared into

scuttled over to Stella, lowering her voice to a whisper. 'I'm afraid my memory is very unreliable, Stella dear. I remember now. You used to be Ross's girlfriend and now you're not.'

'No, I'm not.' Stella hoped her tone would discourage any conversation on the subject.

Lilias didn't take the hint. 'He's such a nice young man.'

'Isn't he.'

'Your granny was so upset when you quarrelled,' Lilias ploughed on. 'But now perhaps you'll make it up again. Wouldn't that be wonderful news for Alice?'

'It won't be happening, I'm afraid.' Stella eased her foot from under a softly snoring Patch. 'Lilias, has Maddie phoned? Did you tell her about Alice's fall?'

Lilias moved away and stood with her back to Stella. 'No, dear. I haven't spoken to Maddie. She's in — '

'Australia. Yes, I know. When she calls I think it would be best if you only mention the broken ankle. Don't say anything about Alice's head.'

'I won't, Stella, I promise, I won't say a word,' Lilias said, like an obedient child.

Stella wondered briefly if she should ask Lilias if she knew why Maddie had gone, but as she didn't have much hope that she would get a sensible response she decided against it. Beside, she had to get on her way without any more delays. 'I'm going upstairs for a photo from Alice's bedroom,' she told Lilias. 'There's one she keeps in a frame on her dressing table. I thought it would be nice for her to have something of her own in with her.'

She didn't linger in Alice's room. It seemed intrusive to be there for one thing, and upsetting. The smells in it were evocative — the cedar-wood trunk Alice kept bed linen in, and the heavy perfume she wore on special occasions, almost conjured up her physical presence. Stella rummaged quickly for a couple of nighties in the chest of drawers — what a conglomeration of stuff there was in the top drawer — and a cardigan to act as a bed jacket, picked up a pair of slippers and a hairbrush, seized the photograph and ran downstairs, afraid of meeting Ross on the landing.

Near the foot of the stairs she came to a stop, arrested by the sight of a painting she'd never seen before. This must be the one that was inadvertently the cause of Alice's fall.

In an abstract style of predominantly glowing yellows and vibrant greens, it showed, unmistakably, Hill View on an evening in early summer.

She walked down slowly towards the painting, not taking her eyes off it. The house disappeared into the thick, confident brush strokes. Who would have thought Lilias capable of this? She felt rather shaken. If she'd thought about the painting at all after first hearing about it, she would have imagined a rather amateur watercolour. Not this mesmerising oil that drew her right into the heart of itself.

She took a few steps back and Hill View emerged again. How wonderful it would be to have this in her room in London.

She pulled her eyes away, went into the sitting room and quickly scanned the bookshelves by the fireplace, remembering their granny reading aloud to Maddie and herself, Alice in the wing chair, the girls on the fireside rug with a dog or a cat sharing the warmth. She picked out two books that Alice particularly loved which had become favourites of theirs too. Glancing inside one she saw that she had written her name in block capitals and, underneath, Hill View, Eildon Street, Melrose, the Borders, Scotland, Great Britain, Europe, the Earth, the Universe.

She was so sure then of her place in the great scheme of things.

Lilias came into the hall as Stella packed the books and photo into her bag and filled

Bette's holdall with the clothes.

'I think your painting's amazing,' Stella said, indicating it. If she were Alice or Maddie she would discuss the technicalities of it but she didn't know how to do that. She only knew that she felt its power and found it hard to connect with the little woman ineffectually dusting a table crammed with nick-nacks, but of course she could hardly say that to Lilias.

'Ross put it up for me,' Lilias said, as he came downstairs. 'It's so heavy. He said we should never have tried to do it ourselves.'

Stella ignored Ross's presence and picked up her bags. 'Well, I think it's wonderful. And let's hope Alice will be home to see it very soon.' She had to put one bag down again to put an arm around the older woman and give her a hug.

'Oh Stella, dear, wait a moment. I have something for Alice, for you to take to her. It's some of my fruit cake, she's so fond of it.'

Lilias darted through to the kitchen and came back with a large square tin with a picture of Edinburgh Castle on the lid. For goodness' sake! Stella bit her tongue, knelt down and tried without success to fit the tin into the tartan holdall.

'Is all this yours?' Ross indicated the two bags, her handbag, and the tin. 'Don't you think it would be easier if you came in the car?'

Stella rose from the floor, feeling foolish and at a disadvantage.

'All right,' she said ungraciously, not wanting to argue the matter in front of Lilias.

Ross lifted the holdall, said goodbye to Lilias, and strode off down the corridor.

I'll grab the holdall once we're outside, Stella thought. I don't care how long I have to wait at the bus stop. But by the time she caught up with Ross he'd put the bag in the back of his car, left the passenger door open and got into the driver's seat.

Coming up the street she could see several neighbours, people who would exclaim over her appearance in the town after a long absence, people who would want to ask after her granny, people she would not want to witness a scene outside Alice's house.

She climbed into the car and pulled the door shut with a bang.

Ross turned the key in the ignition and put the car into gear. His right-hand knuckles looked white as he clenched his fingers round the steering wheel. If anyone had told him this morning that he'd be this close to Stella Greenlaw, having volunteered to sit beside her for an hour and a half, he'd have said, no way. No way. In fact that was, more or less, what he'd said to his mother when she'd phoned him last night after Stella had gone to bed, ostensibly to ask him how the tasting went but really, he knew, to let him know Stella's plans for the next day. She never said, you could give her a lift back to Edinburgh, but the words somehow conveyed themselves down the line. Eventually, given his lack of response on the subject, she'd stopped talking about Stella and asked for all the details on his successful evening.

But this morning he'd been delayed by the man turning up with the pheasants and the turkeys — otherwise he'd have seen Lilias earlier and been away from Hill View before Stella arrived.

His offer of a lift had been made out of mere politeness, of going through the motions, and he didn't expect her to accept, but when he saw her kneel on the floor to wrestle with that ridiculous Edinburgh Castle tin his conscience smote him and he'd renewed the offer before he could stop himself.

Fate was conspiring against him. But he tried to tell himself that it wasn't a big deal. He was only giving her a lift.

He'd looked at her left hand when they were sitting at the table in Alice's kitchen. No ring. But that didn't mean there was nobody in her life. Some smooth-talking London whizz kid. Someone she looked at the way she used to look at him, a glint of mischief in her green eyes.

Her hair was caught up in a clasp at the back of her head. Beneath her jacket she was wearing a smart dress in a sort of caramel colour, looking good enough to eat, and high-heeled shoes, dressed formally as if for a business meeting. No doubt she wished herself anywhere other than here, in his car. No doubt she wished she were back in London, in her new life. Then he remembered the reason she was here and how much Alice meant to her.

He pulled himself together to speak. 'Where do you want to go?'

She turned her head slightly towards him. 'Where are you going? Were you planning to go through town?'

'No, but it's not a problem. If you want to go Maddie's flat I'll take you there, or I could drop you off at the hospital.' The hospital was on the outskirts, on this side of the city, which would suit him perfectly.

'The hospital would be great. It won't be visiting time but I hope they'll let me sit with her anyway — she's in a room on her own.' She turned slightly away, hunching in her seat, leaning away from him.

Okay. If that's the way she wanted to play it — minimum physical and verbal communication — that was absolutely fine with him. What he wanted too. He drove through the town and out into the countryside.

An oncoming driver flashed his lights. Ross's best friend, Gavin Armstrong. Ross acknowledged him with a raise of his hand.

'That was Gav, wasn't it?' Stella lowered her hand and Ross realised that she too had seen their old schoolmate and automatically given the country greeting. Now she looked as if she regretted speaking, but after a moment she asked, 'What's he up to these days?'

'In partnership in the garage with his dad. And he and Carol have had a baby.'

'I heard from Maddie that she was expecting. I didn't know it had arrived.'

'Well, how could you know? You haven't been here.' Now why had he said that, and in that tone of voice? Better to pretend that they were merely old acquaintances without much to say to each other. And much better not to remember Gav and Carol's wedding dance and walking Stella home under the stars afterwards. So sure that they were happy together . . .

Stella flinched but he couldn't bring himself to apologise.

He expected her to look away again but she asked, 'Boy or girl?'

'Can't remember. One or the other, I expect.' He grinned at her without meaning to, and looked away quickly.

'Ross.' Stella cleared her throat. 'I know this is difficult. I know you'd rather I wasn't here, in the car I mean. But as I am can you please tell me what on earth is going on with Maddie? You took her to the airport?'

This was safer ground. 'Yes. Alice asked if I would. See that she got off in one piece. You know what your wee sister's like. Quite likely to turn up a day late or join the wrong queue for departures. Like that time she — '

But Stella was not to be deflected. 'And she was going to Sydney, Bette said?'

'Sydney,' Ross confirmed briefly. Why had he started chatting away about Maddie like he would have done before? Reminding them both about how much their lives had been entwined for so long.

'But why?'

Ross checked the rear-view mirror before slowing down. How much should he tell her? And how much did he know for sure anyway? Maddie had spilled it all out but he'd been concentrating on getting through the late afternoon traffic on the way to the airport, plus it sounded as if she didn't understand it properly herself. And there was Skye in the back seat, excited on Maddie's behalf, the two of them chattering away like birds on a wire.

'Mum and Grandpa know, I think, but they say it's up to Alice to tell you,' he said. 'There was some family fall-out years ago or something. I know that's not much help but Alice will be the best person to ask.'

He risked a glance at her. She was hanging on his words, the previous flinty expression in her eyes gone. He had a mad urge to stop the car and take her in his arms.

A toot from behind made him accelerate.

'A family fall-out?'

'I thought it was crazy,' he said, 'Maddie going, not you. But Maddie said of course you were so busy at work and anyway you don't like flying and Alice would phone you after she left and it would all be a lovely surprise for you. But then, I suppose, Alice must have had her accident before she could do that.'

'A lovely surprise?' Stella echoed.

'I remember she said it was something to do with Alice's family. Not the Greenlaws, but Alice's own family.'

'But she doesn't have any. I remember an old aunt on our grandfather's side but nobody on Alice's. This gets odder and odder.'

90

'I don't think there's much else I can tell you.' He thought of something, not that it would answer any of her questions though. 'We didn't just drop her off, of course. We went into the terminal building with her, as far as we could go. She should definitely have got on that plane.'

'Right.' She slumped in her seat, staring ahead.

To fill the silence, Ross turned on the radio. The news was ending with a financial bulletin.

He turned the dial to find the country music programme. No! That wasn't a good idea. The two of them used to love to sing along in the car to cheesy ballads, adapting the words to being about themselves or their friends, but joint rewriting of lyrics was hardly a way they could pass the time today. He smiled grimly to himself at the thought. Dolly Parton, eat your heart out.

'What was that? Did you hear it? About InsideOut?' Stella was sitting bolt upright.

'What do you mean? On the news?'

She leaned forward to turn the dial back. Their hands collided briefly before she moved hers away as if she'd been stung. 'Can we try and get another news programme?'

'Stella, what on earth is it?' he asked, aware that he was using her name for the first time today. At least he hadn't come out with 'Star', his own special name for her.

'I don't know. I just heard 'InsideOut'.'

'What about them?'

'It's the job I'm working on at the moment.' She pushed her hands through her hair. 'Nothing's supposed to have been announced yet. Something must have gone wrong.'

Ross scanned the road ahead and then crossed over, turned into a driveway and switched off the engine. 'Not necessarily. Calm down.'

She put her head in her hands. 'How can I calm down?' Her voice sounded as if it were coming through clenched teeth. 'Something must have gone wrong with the deal. I should be there. But how can I go back now? I must be with Alice.'

Ross was quiet, hoping she would interpret the silence as a sympathetic one, but his mind was blank. What could she do? No one could be in two places at once. 'Is there anyone you can call?' he asked eventually. 'In your office?'

She fumbled in her bag for her mobile. 'I'll try Pete's direct line,' she said. 'He's my boss.' She scrolled down the contact list, hit the green button and put the phone to her ear. 'It's gone to voicemail. I'll try . . . I'll try Nathan. He's taken the deal over from me for now.'

And does he mean anything else to you? Ross wanted to ask. There had been a slight change of tone in her voice and her face had flushed when she'd said his name. Nathan. Stella and Nathan. Well, he'd have to get used to it. If it weren't this Nathan guy it would be someone else. He couldn't expect that she'd be short of male company — and it was her who broke up their relationship, he reminded himself. He found his fingernails were digging painfully into his palm.

Evidently *Nathan* wasn't answering either.

'I can't remember Pete's PA's extension.' Stella shook the phone in frustration. 'I'll have to go through the main switchboard.' Her hand was shaking as she held the phone to her ear, and her eyes were shut, as if she were willing someone at the other end to tell her everything was all right.

'Jane, hi. It's Stella. Is Pete there? Nathan? Right. Could you ask one of them to ring me as soon as they get back? Thanks.'

She dropped the phone into her lap. 'Not sure what's going on. One of my colleagues was supposed to go to a meeting on my behalf yesterday. It must be serious if Pete's got involved.'

'Well, there's nothing you can do.'

'I know that but it doesn't help.'

93

Ross looked around, hoping to find inspiration for what he might say next. 'Do you know where we are?' He pointed up the driveway.

Stella craned her neck to the right. 'Thirlestane Castle. I haven't been there for years.'

'It's shut for the winter or else we could have gone for a coffee.'

'Coffee?' She could hear her voice rising.

'There's Carfraemill down the road. It'll be open. If you don't want to, that's fine. But it would take away the taste of that concoction of Lilias's.'

She didn't look at him but he could see the corner of her mouth quirk up. 'Won't it make you late?'

He took that as a yes. 'Half an hour won't make much difference.'

He'd made the gesture because she looked so miserable — it didn't seem fair that she had problems at work on top of worrying about Alice. But it was a stressful job that she had made the decision to take, he reminded himself, and he wasn't in a position to console her the way he once would have done. Already regretting the suggestion, he drove on to Carfraemill.

★ ★ ★

It was a shame that it was off-season for Thirlestane. Stella remembered a school trip there and being thrilled by the fairy-tale castle and its vast green velvet lawns. Of course Ross was on that trip too — they were probably aged about thirteen or fourteen, at the stage when they kept their after-school friendship apart from their school life. Ross, just beginning to take rugby seriously, was the same height as herself then. A couple of years later he towered over her and their paths diverged as all of his spare time was taken up with practice.

The kitchen café at Carfraemill was warm and welcoming. Stella put her phone on the table so that she'd be sure not to miss a call but she felt herself relax a little, ready to forget for the moment about the possible problem at work. But it was like a dream — whether a good one or a bad one she couldn't decide — to be here with Ross and no one else. What on earth were they going to talk about? She tucked her legs under her chair so that there was no possibility of her accidentally playing footsie with him.

Maybe Ross was having second thoughts about issuing the invitation. He didn't seem to know what to say either but was staring at the cheerful red Aga in the corner as if it were the most fascinating thing he'd ever seen.

She looked at him covertly. He was in good shape considering he wasn't playing professional sport any more. For a moment she allowed herself to think of the first match he'd played for Scotland. Standing on the terrace with Gav and Carol and a crowd of other friends, she cheered until she was hoarse when he scored a try. She remembered how nice he'd been to the crowd of young lads wanting his autograph afterwards.

It was a heady time. Then, although Ross was initially devastated when his fledgling international career — his whole rugby career — was cut short after he broke his shoulder, he threw his energies into running the family business. It was certainly no coincidence that Gray chose that time to announce that he wanted to spend more time on the golf course and was handing the reins over to his grandson.

She stole another glance. His dark, almost black, hair was a little longer than it used to be, touching the collar of the jacket he'd pulled on when they got out of the car. Maybe because his rugby-playing days had come to an end prematurely his face didn't bear any of the typical battle scars, no broken nose or misshapen ears.

'You're Ross Drummond, aren't you?' said the pretty waitress as she handed them menus. 'My brother played for Melrose with you.'

They chatted about mutual acquaintances, Ross's face animated and the girl's sparkling in return. Stella couldn't bear to watch them. Of course he wouldn't have taken long in finding another girlfriend — probably a line of hopefuls formed a queue the minute she was out of the picture. She stared at the menu, reading every line, although she wasn't planning on having anything other than coffee.

If only they could go back, as far back as that school trip to Thirlestane Castle, excited about being out of class for the afternoon. Knowing that when she got home Alice would be waiting to hear all about it. Knowing that she and Ross were friends.

'Oh, sorry,' Ross said to Stella, rather belatedly. He introduced the girl. 'And this is Stella.'

Stella handed the menu back. 'Americano, no milk, please.'

'Same, with milk.' Ross returned the waitress's smile. 'Good to see you.'

That smile was like a stab to the heart — although of course she had only herself to blame; she'd forfeited the right to be looked at like that by Ross Drummond. Was he enjoying playing the field or was he having a

. . . a thing with Skye? She'd said that she was going down to Melrose tomorrow, hadn't she? Why else would she be going other than to see Ross? To spend the nights with him. One way to find out . . .

'I met Maddie's flat — ' she began.

'I was thinking — ' Ross said at the same time. 'Sorry, go on, what were you going to say?'

She shook her head. Thank goodness he'd interrupted — did she really think that he'd discuss Skye with her? And could she have borne it if he had? Anyway, no doubt she'd find out soon enough if there was something serious between them. 'It doesn't matter. What were you thinking?' It was an awkwardly intimate thing to be asking.

Ross gestured towards the Aga. 'It looks good, doesn't it? Cosy. Perhaps Alice could get one? That range of hers is pretty hopeless.'

Well, it certainly wasn't an intimate answer.

'Agas are expensive, aren't they? Alice couldn't afford one.'

'It was just a thought. Something will have to be done. The old range isn't going to last much longer. You don't want it grinding to a halt in the winter.'

'I'll look into it.' Flaking paintwork, missing tiles, and now this. No one knew the state of Alice's finances better than Stella.

There was no money to spend on an Aga or on any other home improvements.

'And I don't know if you noticed but Hill View's got some roof tiles missing — and water's come through into the attic space. Lilias sent me up there — she thought she could hear rats.'

'Rats!'

'Don't worry, it wasn't — a bird had got in and couldn't get out again, poor thing. I put buckets under the drips but some of the stuff up there got wet.'

'I'll look into that too.'

Her voice must have had an edge to it that she hadn't intended because Ross said, 'Keep your hair on. I know a few tradesmen if you need any recommendations.'

'I'll bear that in mind.'

The coffee was strong and good and banished any lingering traces of Lilias's strange-tasting tea. She searched her mind for a different topic of conversation. Perhaps 'do you remember' was a dangerous opening but it was all she could come up with.

'Do you remember that school trip to Thirlestane?'

'Not sure I appreciated it at that age,' he said. 'But I've been in the castle a few times lately. We do some private catering. My chef's full of good ideas — that was one of them.'

She'd love to know more about that but she wasn't going to ask.

'Is Bette minding the shop today?' Silly question. Of course Bette was at home this morning, after shop-opening time.

He put down his mug and stretched out his long legs, pulling them back as they coincided with Stella's.

'Sorry. She'll probably pop in at some point, rearrange the shelves to her satisfaction, but I've got a full-time assistant in the deli now, Gav's sister. There's the restaurant too — tons more paperwork and I can't be in both places at once.'

She wasn't going to pursue that either. She didn't want to know more about how his business was doing, the business they might have run together.

'And your work?' He sounded as remote as if they'd met as strangers at a dinner party. 'You enjoy it? At least, when it's not inadvertently getting mentioned on the news?'

'I've had some interesting assignments — the current one is a management buy-out,' she said. 'It's vital it works out otherwise there'll be job losses.'

He blew out his lips. Almost like a kiss. 'Big stuff then,' he said, unconsciously echoing his grandfather's reaction. If this were before, when she was in the Edinburgh office, he'd have asked questions, wanted to hear more. But now, like herself, he seemed unwilling to respond to her replies in a way that would turn this into a proper conversation. He reached into his jacket pocket for his wallet. 'Perhaps we should get on.'

'Let me get this.' Stella gestured to him to put his money away. 'As a thank you for the lift.'

He stood up, pushing his chair back so that it scraped along the floor. 'I may not be earning mega bucks in the Big City but I can afford to buy you a coffee.'

They stared at each other.

Was this it? Stella's heart pounded. Was this the showdown she'd been half-expecting from the moment she got into the car? She looked away first, biting her lip to stop it trembling. 'I didn't mean that. I just — '

The waitress was back. 'Did you enjoy your coffee?'

Stella got to her feet. 'Yes, thank you,' she said. 'Could you tell me where the Ladies is, please?' She lifted her phone and her purse and left the café without looking back.

In the cloakroom she stared at herself in the mirror.

Ambitious girl keen to get on in her career, not letting anything — or anyone — stand in her way. That's how Ross must have interpreted her decision to move to London.

The real story was much more complicated.

* * *

Stella drank in the countryside as they drove in silence through it.

During the drive in the dark the previous evening she hadn't seen the wind farm, an alien presence in this landscape and yet strangely wonderful too, an army of mythical giants waving their arms.

The Eildon Hills were white on the top, like a snow queen's tablecloth. It was said that fairies lived there and that long ago the Queen of the Fairies enticed a Borders man called Thomas the Rhymer away to fairyland. When he returned years later — thinking he'd been gone only a few days — he had the ability to see into the future. Alice read Stella and Maddie that story one winter when they were little and for years they imagined that their Christmas-tree fairy had come from that fairyland in the hills.

The seasons all had something special here. Impossible to say which was best. Leafless trees stark against the sky in winter. In autumn their foliage blazed orange and gold, and the sun filtered through them into the crisp mornings. In spring the daffodils carpeted the garden at Hill View and lambs played in the surrounding farms. And on a warm summer's day, the town's gardens were jewel-bright while in the burn below the house, when they were children, they sat dangling their feet in the water.

There was nowhere in the world like the Borders . . .

If she'd stayed here, she and Ross would still be together, might even be engaged.

She'd been going to wait until the day after Gav and Carol's wedding to tell him about the job in London but as they were walking back to Hill View afterwards he pulled her close, picked confetti out of her hair and told her he loved her. Wondering if he was going to seize the moment to mention marriage in connection with themselves, she jumped in to forestall him. It seemed wrong to continue the evening as if nothing was going to change.

As they came to the square she'd released her hand from his. 'Can we sit down? I've got something to tell you.'

He tried to take her hand again. 'What is it?'

'Let's sit here.' It would be easier if she didn't have to look at him.

He put his arm along the bench behind her

and gazed up at the sky. 'Starry starry night,' he sang, 'and Stella-star-of-the-sea beside me. What more could I want?' He would certainly never get picked to sing for Scotland, something she often teased him about. But not tonight.

She moved slightly forward so that he wasn't touching her. 'I've been offered a new job.'

'Promotion? Which department?'

'Investment.'

'You kept that quiet — that you were applying for it. That's excellent. When do you start?'

'Three weeks.'

He put his arm round her and kissed the top of her head. 'Congratulations!' When she didn't respond he said, 'Hey, not having second thoughts, are you? You don't sound too thrilled. You'll be brilliant at it.'

'It's in the London office. I didn't apply for it. They came to me. I hope it'll only be for a couple of years.'

'London! What do you mean? Is this a wind-up?'

She stood up facing him, and tried to look him in the eye. Failing that, she stared at the ground, scuffing it with her green sandal.

'I'm moving to London. It's a good opportunity and I've accepted it.'

'London!' he said again. 'But why the heck didn't you discuss it with me? You never said a word. Three weeks! I can't believe it. When were you going to tell me?'

'I am telling you. But I don't plan — '

'Are you breaking up with me, Stella?' The look in his eyes was very hard to bear.

'No,' she said in anguish. 'No. It's just something I need to do.'

'Something that doesn't involve me.' He stood up now. 'I never thought this is how the night would end.' He rubbed his forehead. 'Maybe I could get a job in London too — put the restaurant plan on hold, find someone to manage the shop.'

She wouldn't let him turn his life upside down, leave Gray in the lurch. Not when she couldn't let him know the truth about why she was going.

'How would that work? No, don't, we can — '

'Can what? How can we have a relationship when you can't tell me about something as monumental as this?'

'Don't shout.'

'I'll shout if I want. Or is it only you who gets her own way?'

'I'm not. It's not like that.'

'Who's shouting now?'

'I'm going home,' she said. If she didn't

leave now, she'd howl like a dog in the moonlight. She gathered up the skirts of her long dress. 'I'll ... I'll text you in the morning, shall I?'

'Do what you like. You're good at that.' Before she could move he'd marched off in the opposite direction.

Now, they hadn't exchanged a word since she'd got back into the car. He must be remembering that night too. A glimpse in the rear-view mirror showed his face with that closed expression she'd grown used to since this morning. Shutting her out.

The panorama of Edinburgh, with Arthur's Seat in the distance, spread out in front of them as they dropped down into the south side of the city. At the traffic lights near the hospital entrance, Ross said stiffly, 'The parking's difficult. I'll stop at the front if I can.'

'Of course.' She gathered up her handbag, shoulder bag and the cake tin. For all its size it didn't feel as if there was much cake in it. But how could she have refused to take it?

Cars were definitely not encouraged to wait at the entrance for more than a few seconds. As Ross braked, another car drove up behind them. Stella got out quickly, ducked her head back in to mumble thanks, and shut the door.

She fought an urge to run after him, to

signal to him to come back, to explain
. . . Instead, she headed into the hospital,
wondering with a return of dread how Alice
was.

5

She came round an hour ago and spoke to us, Stella was told at the nurses' station. The motherly nurse smiled at her when she sank onto a chair, weak with relief.

'Not out of the woods yet, love, but it's hopeful,' she said. 'She's sleeping but you can go and sit with her.'

Alice lay as still as she had yesterday but her cheeks were a healthier colour, Stella thought, as she switched her phone to silent. She took her grandmother's hand and held it to her face for a moment.

The cake tin wouldn't fit in the bedside locker so had to sit on top — its picture of Edinburgh Castle a reminder of one of the happiest days of her life.

She and Ross had been showing visiting friends around the city and as they were all admiring the view from the castle wall he had suddenly taken her arm and walked her out of earshot.

'I love you,' he'd whispered in her ear.

'I did suspect that,' she answered, teasingly. 'What brought this on now?'

'I couldn't wait another minute to tell you.

I suspect you feel the same but I'd be glad if you confirmed it.'

'I can confirm it.' She kissed him back as proof of the statement, to calls of 'You two, get a room' from their friends.

Now, on the cake tin lid, she traced her finger down to where she thought they had been standing that day.

The nurse came in with a jug of water. 'Sorry, dear. We can't have the locker-top cluttered up. I'm afraid you'll have to take the tin away.'

Stella looked inside, at the small hunk of fruitcake wrapped in greaseproof paper. Feeling guilty she put it in the bin.

'Is it all right to have this?' She took out the frame. 'I thought it would be nice for my granny to see when she wakes up.'

'Lovely idea. Let's have a look. Is that you?'

'And my sister,' Stella said.

The photo showed Alice with Stella and Maddie when they were about five and two, so it must have been taken very soon after their parents' accident, when they went to live with her in Melrose. They were sitting on the sand somewhere, somewhere windy as Alice's hair blew around her face. The girls wore sunhats.

'Lovely,' the nurse said again. 'Well, I'll leave you alone now.'

Who took the photo? Stella wondered. Gray probably. She must ask him. She turned the frame over. The back was quite flimsy and it was easy to slip the picture out.

'Coldingham Sands' was written in Alice's sloping and beautifully clear script. Stella couldn't recall the occasion even with that clue but then it was more than twenty years ago. Maddie had no recollection at all of those early days with Alice. Perhaps it was as well that Stella herself could only remember fragments from the time when their lives had altered so drastically.

Asking where Mummy and Daddy were. Finally understanding that they wouldn't be coming back. She only had hazy memories of their parents now — but were they real memories or inspired by the photograph album Alice showed them? She didn't know.

Funny little memories of those early days. The smell of Alice's Pear's Soap. Running up and down the back corridor. Being alarmed by Alice's dog, Patch's predecessor — he loomed up at them like a big black monster until they realised what a softy he was. Alice telling her that her name meant star-of-the-sea. Years later she told Ross that, and 'Star' became his pet name for her.

Stella leaned over the woman who had brought them up, who'd made a happy life for them, and stroked her hair, still silvery fair. 'Thank you for taking care of us,' she whispered.

Since she moved to London she'd started to realise how much her granny's life had changed with the death of her only son and his wife, when the little granddaughters, staying with her while their parents were on holiday, had to remain with her. Widowed — her husband had been fifteen years older than her — she might have married again, or travelled to see the world's best art galleries, or had a major exhibition of her own work, or . . . but what was the point of speculating?

The hospital nightie she was wearing was clean but threadbare — oh no! Too late Stella remembered the holdall on the back seat of Ross's car with Alice's own clothes in it. She could ask Gray to bring it up — he'd definitely be coming to see Alice when she was allowed more visitors, but who knew when that would be? She'd have to do some shopping.

Delving into her bag again she took out the books she'd chosen from the bookshelf at Hill View: *The Thirty-Nine Steps* and *Little Women*. She'd anticipated reading them aloud to an unconscious Alice in the hope that a familiar voice would get through, but happily that wasn't necessary now. So instead she opened the first page of John Buchan's famous novel and got quietly immersed in it herself. The minute she read the first line, 'I returned from the City about three o'clock on that May afternoon pretty well disgusted with life', it took her back to the first time Alice had read the book to Maddie and herself. Alice was wonderful at reading aloud and when she told them that the author once lived not very far from Melrose, that made the book all the more special.

A couple of hours later Alice was still asleep.

The nurse she'd seen earlier popped her head round the door and beckoned her to come out.

'He said he didn't want to disturb you but I thought you'd want to see him,' she said, giving Stella a complicit smile.

'Who?'

Ross stood by the nurses' station, the tartan holdall in his hand. He held it out at arm's length as if to avoid any contact with her. 'Found this when I was loading up the car at Costit.'

'It was good of you to bring it.' Stella kept her eyes on the bag as she took it from him.

'How's Alice?' he asked.

'She's regained consciousness. She's sleep-ing now — I haven't spoken to her.' Now she

112

had to look at him. 'But she has come round, that's the main thing. Please tell Gray for me — and could you possibly let Lilias know? I don't know if she can hear the phone. She's never answered it when I've called.'

He nodded his acknowledgement at the good news about Alice. 'Excellent. I'll tell them.'

She couldn't help continuing to keep her eyes on him, as if she were memorising him. Who knew when she would see him again? That little dip, not quite a dimple, in his cheek when he smiled. A hint of dark stubble on his chin — he mustn't have had time to shave this morning. His height; she was five foot seven in her heels and was only just as high as his shoulder. How could she have thought that going out with Nathan would make her forget him? Nathan — at this moment she could hardly recall anything about him.

'I'll be off then.' Without any further ado Ross was away — no doubt anxious to put distance between them. She watched him go, until he turned at the end of the corridor and disappeared.

The nurse reappeared. 'Oh, he's gone.' Her mouth turned down at the corners. Perhaps she'd been hoping to witness a romantic scene. 'Your boyfriend? Who's a lucky girl!'

'No, he's . . . he just gave me a lift. Can I stay a bit longer with my granny?'

''Course you can, love. And when she wakes, if you're not here, we'll tell her you've been. And you ring us any time. Grannies are special, aren't they — I'm one myself!'

Her understanding and friendliness were warming.

Back in Alice's room she was mortified to see that the nighties she'd grabbed in such haste were hardly in any better condition that the hospital-issued one, and the slippers were an ancient furry pair, half-chewed by Patch in his younger days. Highly dangerous for someone who was going to be unsteady on her feet for the next few months. She put them in the bin, along with the nighties. But even when it was empty the holdall couldn't stretch to accommodate the Edinburgh Castle tin. Great. She was going to look like a bag lady on the bus.

She waited another hour, until her stomach growled, reminding her it was now some time since her breakfast toast. Kissing Alice, she tiptoed out of the room.

Down in the lobby she checked her phone. A text message and a missed call.

Nathan. *Stella-Bella hope all good with you, call me?*

But what would she say? She moved on to

the voicemail. Pete's PA. *Stella, hi, it's Jane. Pete's asked me to say he'll ring you later but no worries. His exact words! Hope your granny's getting better. Bye.*

No worries. She couldn't help smiling. In her head she could hear Pete booming his favourite expression.

But if only she had 'no worries'. Since that phone call from Lilias the night before last it felt as if all her worries had come at once.

*   *   *

'So, how was it?' Bette helped Ross tidy away dry goods into the storeroom at the back of the restaurant.

'How was what?' Ross knew he was fruitlessly playing for time with the question. Of course his mother wasn't asking him about the traffic or the cash-and-carry.

'How was Stella?'

Yup. That was what he'd been expecting to hear. 'How did you know I'd seen her?'

'Gav came into the shop. Asked if that was really Stella he saw with you this morning. How was it?' his mother asked again.

'Fine. No big deal.'

'Did you meet her at Hill View? Did you have a good talk?'

'She came in just as I'd got the range

going. We talked. About nothing very much. And we stopped at Carfraemill for coffee.' He might as well confess that now — no doubt Bette would hear about it on the bush telegraph before the day was over.

He'd regretted what he said about paying for the coffee the minute the words were out of his mouth and he saw Stella's stricken expression. So much for playing it cool.

And he'd have to tell Bette about returning the bag to Stella in the hospital — in fact he should have told her right away that Alice had regained consciousness.

'That's wonderful,' Bette said when he'd finished confessing. 'I'll ring your grandfather.'

Left alone, Ross thought back to sitting with Stella in the café. For a moment he'd almost forgotten how it was between them, almost got sucked into the useless game of 'do you remember?'

No. Concentrating on what was ahead, not behind him, was what he had to do now.

He should try to look on today in a positive way. Closure — wasn't that the way to put it? Perhaps he should try internet dating — he had a friend who met a lovely woman that way. And before her, several other lovely women. Or maybe he should think about pursuing a relationship with Skye. She was pretty and good fun. He'd called to see Maddie one evening in September to go through her accounts and found that she'd forgotten their arrangement and was away at a craft trade fair. Skye offered him a drink and he ended up spending the night with her — 'no strings' she'd said and that suited him just fine.

If Isabel was aware he'd stayed — she'd come in late and he left very early — she gave no sign of it.

But he wasn't sure if Skye really meant 'no strings', which was why he was apprehensive about her coming down here for two nights. He didn't seem to be able to figure girls out any more, the way he could before he and Stella were together. Seemed to have lost the knack of recognising signals, of decoding words that said one thing but meant something else.

Skye could sleep in the flat upstairs and he'd go home to Gray's. He didn't want to be the subject of gossip — the downside of living in a small community — as had happened after Stella left. The shop had never been so busy than in the first few days after; he was sure people came in just to see how he was taking it.

Anyway, this was the way it would be from now on — if he'd ever, deep deep down, harboured any hope of reconciliation with Stella, it was gone now. The future was Ross Drummond running the family business here in Melrose, and Stella Greenlaw making deals in the City of London, with nearly four hundred miles between them. All their shared past gone, like yesterday's rainbow.

And other things were going to change. He had plans to open up part of the deli as somewhere people could sit, well, four people anyway. Café was too grand a word for it, but Gav's sister would make fresh scones every morning and learn how to work a machine that made several varieties of coffee for people to drink there or take away, and they'd put tables on the pavement when the weather was fine.

At home it would be all change too, with his father coming back to Scotland for good and his parents living together in a house of their own for the first time in many years.

'Ross?' Bette was waving her hand in front of his face. 'Hello? Anyone there?'

'Sorry, Mum. Right. Let's get the rest of the stuff put away and then I must go and see Tom.'

'Everything sorted for when he's away?'

'Hope so. Tom's are big shoes to fill.'

People came from far and wide to try Tom's cooking and, as he'd said, they were fully booked tonight and tomorrow. But of course he couldn't miss his niece's wedding.

Perhaps it was the reminder of the reason for Tom's absence that brought Bette back to her earlier topic of conversation. Clearly she was not going to give up. 'You should get Stella to eat in the restaurant sometime.'

'Mum. That's not going to happen. Please can you drop the subject?'

'I'm sorry, darling. It's just . . . oh, well, the world is full of what-might-have-beens. And it is almost Christmas.'

'What's that got to do with it? Life isn't a film. This story won't have a soppy ending with everyone wearing Santa hats.' Stella loved romantic comedies, especially Christmas ones, and he'd loved her enough to sit through them. Santa hats featured rather a lot, he seemed to remember.

Bette rolled her eyes at him. 'Your grandpa's over the moon about Alice. I'll go and see Lilias now in case she hasn't heard from Stella.'

Ross grinned at her. 'Whatever you do, say no if she offers you herbal tea.'

Bette opened the door then turned back. 'I've decided to cancel the party.'

'Cancel it! What will the neighbours do on Christmas Eve? They'll have to roam the streets of Melrose trying to find somebody else to entertain them.'

His mother made a face at his teasing, hovering half in and half out of the shop. 'Postpone it, I should say. It wouldn't be the same without Alice — and to think of her in hospital while we're having fun. If she's home we'll have it on Hogmanay instead.'

Maybe she'd forgotten that Alice wasn't at last year's Christmas Eve party either although of course for a different reason, spending Christmas in Edinburgh with Stella and Maddie. He'd put in a token appearance himself and then gone for a pint or two with Gav.

When Bette had gone he went upstairs to the flat. He needed to start getting it ready while he had some spare time, for Skye's visit tomorrow. What a mess everything was, including this flat, his home for the last thirteen months — the watery afternoon sun showed up the marks on the white woodchip wallpaper here in the sitting room. The whole place hadn't seen a fresh coat of paint for at least thirty years.

Bette had wanted to give the place a complete makeover before he moved in but he couldn't see the point. If it had been for Stella and himself, that would have been quite different. They'd put in a modern kitchen and bathroom, choose colours, he'd ask Gav to help him rewire the place . . . soft moody lighting . . . a new double bed . . . But Stella had never set foot in the place.

He should do something about it though, he thought, casting a critical eye round. He'd replaced the fridge when it expired a few months ago but otherwise everything was what had been left by the previous owner, was dated and shabby and hadn't been of good quality to start with. He hadn't told his mother and grandfather yet but he'd decided that when Bette left he'd move back to Priorsford Road to keep Gray company — and to save him from an unwanted housekeeper. He could rent this place out — maybe Tom would want it, save him travelling forty miles there and back every day from his home in the countryside south of Melrose.

The bedroom walls were covered in faded flowery paper and the carpet had seen better days a very long time ago but there was nothing he could do about these things right now. He opened the window to let in some air and fetched fresh bed linen to put beside the bed, ready for tomorrow. How amazing would it be if he were making up the bed for Stella and himself?

And like a wave it came over him, that Christmas Eve three years ago. His mother's annual party. The house full of friends and neighbours. Stella wearing a red dress and earrings like fluffy snowballs. The old-friend kiss under the mistletoe turning into something that took them both by surprise. Slipping away from the party, both of them equally astonished at this change in their relationship. So familiar with each other yet it was as if they had met some new, wonderful person.

The first night they'd spent together. That first morning, and the joy of seeing Stella lying beside him, watching her wake up.

He juggled his first job after his business studies degree and his increasing rugby commitments to meet her in Edinburgh or Melrose. They tried new restaurants, sometimes on their own, sometimes in a crowd. Went to the cinema — although they rarely liked the same film. Had blissful evenings in. Walked in the Border hills.

Then there was the day in early spring, when they'd taken visiting friends out to lunch. Afterwards they'd walked up the Royal Mile onto the ramparts of Edinburgh Castle to show the visitors the view over the city. For the whole of the meal he'd been aware of Stella on the other side of the table, talking and laughing, and as he joined in all he could think was that he loved her. He couldn't wait until they were alone so he put his arms around her up there by the castle wall, oblivious to the proximity of their friends and a few dozen tourists, and whispered the words into her ear. And she said she loved him too.

Later, on their own, they talked about the future. Not mentioning their eventual marriage as such but there it was, unspoken in both their minds. He was sure of that then and was sure of it now. So why . . . If he lived to be a hundred he'd never figure it out.

★　★　★

Stella walked along Abbeyhill Road, wondering what revelations would be in store for her when Peter phoned. He'd said 'no worries' which meant he'd sorted out whatever the problem had been. But she didn't want him to step in, take the whole thing over. Not now. One of the men she was dealing with at InsideOut had been difficult at the start — old-school, prejudiced because she was young and because she was a woman, but she'd won him round. It was her hand on the tiller and she wanted to keep it that way.

She let herself into the flat. All was quiet.

It felt very odd, getting undressed in Maddie's room, taking down the old blue woolly dressing gown from the back of the door and putting it on. She tied her hair back. A shower would be wonderful. She had been too tired last night and in too much of a rush this morning.

She was in the hall, wondering if there were towels in one of the cupboards, when the front door opened.

'Maddie!' It was Skye's surprised voice.

Stella turned round. 'It's Stella. I've borrowed Maddie's dressing gown. Would it be okay if I had a shower? Is there a towel I could use?'

'Here.' Skye opened the door of what proved to be an airing cupboard with a pile of towels on top of the tank. 'You gave me a start! I didn't realise how alike you and Maddie are, although you're taller. She wears that dressing gown a lot.'

Stella rubbed the sleeve. 'It's all pilled. She's had it since she was about fourteen.'

'She calls it her comfort blanket. How's your granny?'

'She's come round but she's not out of the woods yet.'

'So you'll be staying on here?' Skye asked.

'I guess so. Is it a problem? Staying here, I mean?'

'You're welcome. But I'll be at my mum's for Christmas and Isabel's going to her parents. Won't you be lonely?'

Wasn't that the title of a song? 'Lonely this Christmas'. Very melodramatic and self-pitying. She refused to be seen like that. 'It will be odd, I suppose. A different kind of Christmas!' She tried to sound upbeat. 'The important thing is that I'll be near Alice.'

'Isabel will be here tonight and tomorrow night but I'm going down to Melrose tomorrow.'

'Yes, you said.' Stella hoped she didn't sound as squeaky to Skye as she did to herself.

'Did you see Ross last night? Did he tell you about it?'

Tell her what?

'Um.' Stella nodded several times in what she felt was a maniacal fashion. 'Good. I'll have my shower now. Thanks for the towel.'

In the bathroom she lifted her chin, closed her eyes, and let the water run over her face — rather a pathetic trickle compared to the rush produced by the power shower in the flat in London.

So that was it then. Ross and Skye. Of course he hadn't told her. Why should he? It was absolutely none of her business. He'd moved on.

She should try and do the same.

Back in Maddie's bedroom Stella emptied

her suitcase, shaking out her clothes and laying them over the chair. She hadn't, she realised, brought very suitable things with her — work dresses and smart trouser suits and heels were what she'd lived in since going down to London. So she had brought nothing casual and comfortable to wear with her, only the clothes of a girl who'd been almost all work and no play for the last fifteen months.

It was out of the question to borrow Maddie's long skirts — not Stella's style at all. Besides, she and her sister were a different size and shape. Maybe she should buy herself some new casual clothes — but that would be extravagant. She had lots of stuff — jeans, jumpers, boots — back home in Melrose. She should have thought to retrieve them yesterday.

She resisted the temptation to wrap herself in Maddie's old dressing gown, her comfort blanket, and picked out a pair of grey wool trousers and a long-sleeved plum-coloured shirt. Rather than put on the heels again she remembered that there was a pair of sandals in the wardrobe, not exactly seasonal and slightly too big, but she was only going to be walking across the hall for now.

In the kitchen she sat on the sofa and tucked her feet under her. She picked the top magazine from a pile on the floor and flicked through the pages of food articles and recipes. Did it belong to Skye? She rummaged until she found a magazine of more general interest. Of course the travel section would have to have an article on Australia. She flung it back on the floor.

She rubbed her feet. They were cold in the flimsy sandals so she went to see if Maddie had any socks. Her phone was lying on the bed and she saw that she'd missed a call.

'Stella, it's Gray. Have you heard from Maddie? Don't worry, she's absolutely fine. I've had an email, don't recognise the address. *Hi Gray and everybody,*' Gray read out, '*I'm really here Down Under! Tried ringing Alice but she must be gadding about!* Exclamation mark. *Charlie and his family are brilliant!!* Two exclamation marks this time. *Please can you tell Alice he was overjoyed to hear all about her. I love Coolharbour, it's really cool!* Exclamation mark. *I'll keep trying to Phone A.*' Gray cleared his throat. '*Has she told Stella about Charlie yet? I'm dying to talk to her about him. Lots of love, Maddie.*

Hope that sets your mind at rest, lassie,' Gray finished with.

What? Stella had been hoping for some clarification of why Maddie had gone to Australia. Was this it? Was Charlie the relative Ross and Skye had vaguely heard about? Or did hearing his name beg more questions than answers? She was about to call Gray back when Isabel phoned.

'I was wondering what your plans were for the evening, Stella? What were you going to eat? The cupboards are bare but I can do some shopping before I come home. Then I'm going out — staff Christmas do.'

'Oh, no, don't, please, you've been so great already, Isabel. I'm going to the hospital. I'll pick something up to eat when I get back.' She sat down on the bed. 'Isabel, Maddie's emailed Gray. She says she's having a good time with someone called Charlie. Do you know who he is?'

'Sort of. I really don't know very much and it's not my family but it doesn't seem fair that you're completely in the dark. I'll tell you what I can when I see you, shall I?'

At last maybe there was the possibility of some sort of explanation.

Another call. Pete this time.

'Pete, what's going on?'

'There's nothing to worry about, Stella.' Her boss's voice was his professional one. 'Your man was playing silly beggars, that's all, refusing to talk to Nathan. I told him you would be back on the case as soon as possible and that Nathan was the go-to until then. The three of us have had a Skype call, which went well — thanks to your excellent groundwork. Nothing will happen now until after Christmas, probably not until January.'

Pete never played games with his staff. If that's what he said the situation was, Stella believed him. And he wasn't cutting her out; despite her current absence he trusted her to see it through.

His voice changed, became more personal. 'And how are things up there in Bonnie Scotland?'

'My grandmother's come round but she's still very woozy and she has a broken ankle.'

'She'll be all the better for seeing you. Anything I can do, make sure you tell me?'

'Thanks,' Stella said gratefully. She was about to say goodbye when a thought struck her. 'Pete, have you heard of somewhere in Australia, maybe near Sydney, called Coolharbour?'

'Yeah, small town to the south,' Pete said. 'Sort of artists' colony I believe. You know, all craft shops and veggie cafés.'

Stella laughed. It must be the same place — Maddie's idea of heaven.

'Why do you want to know? Thinking of emigrating?'

'My sister's gone there but I don't know why and of course I can't ask my granny yet. It's all a bit of a mystery.'

'I can probably find someone who knows someone from Coolharbour if you want some detective work done.'

'I might take you up on that,' said Stella. 'Bye, Pete.'

'Oh, hang on. Have you spoken to young Nathan? He's been as cheerful as a wet weekend in Wagga Wagga since he found out you'd gone home. Put him out of his misery, will you?'

Stella laughed at his British/Australian mash-up. 'I will do,' she promised. She knew it wasn't something she could put off any longer so as soon as Pete had hung up she steeled herself to make the call.

'Stella-Bella!' She could hear Nathan pushing his chair back. Now he was on the move, probably going to stand where she had on Monday, away from the ears of colleagues. 'How's it going up there?'

She told him briefly about Alice.

'That's the pits,' he said. 'Poor old you. Wish I was nearer, could give you a hug.'

'Thanks, Nat.' Life would be much better if she genuinely wished that too. 'Pete's filled me in on what happened yesterday.'

'He was a tricky one, that InsideOut guy. 'I will deal only with Miss Greenlaw',' Nathan mimicked. 'I found myself outside his door before I'd said two words. However, we've pacified him. He'll stay in his cage until the wonderful Miss Greenlaw returns.'

Stella laughed. 'His bark is worse than his bite when you know him better. Listen, take care, Nathan, have a good Christmas — well, I know you will, with your friends in that lovely house you showed me.'

'I'm sorry you won't be there. We'll get together soon, yeah?'

'I'm not sure yet when I'll be back. I'll let you know.'

There was a pause. 'Do that. Keep in touch, Stella-Bella.'

Some caffeine was urgently needed. A gin and tonic would be even better, if she'd had some to hand. Just as well she hadn't; she needed to keep a clear head. So coffee it was and some mindless late-afternoon television before it was time to leave for the Infirmary.

6

Mam sinks down to sit on the pavement, pulling Alice with her.

'Can you read it for me?' she says to the boy, her voice almost a whisper.

He stares at her.

'Go on,' says Mam fiercely. 'Please.'

Carefully, the boy opens the telegram.

He reads what is written there, mouthing the words to himself. Then he looks down at Mam and Alice, grinning.

'It's from someone called Jack, missus. He's coming home on leave, Thursday week. All my dear love Jack, he says.'

Da is handsome and kind, exactly as Mam said.

He isn't black and white like in the photograph. His eyes are brown, like Alice's. His uniform is the colour of Alice's scratchy cardie but the buttons are shiny and he has a cap he lets Alice try on. He doesn't have a moustache any more.

Alice still loves Uncle Frank best but now she loves Da too.

Da, Mam and Alice have five lovely days together. Da carries Alice on his shoulders and they walk all the way round the town like that and Alice waves to everybody. Uncle Frank brings them a second-hand gramophone and Da puts on some music and dances with Alice round and round the house and out into the street while Mam laughs and laughs.

They take some stale crusts of bread up to the duck pond in the park but all the ducks have gone — someone's had a nice roast for dinner, Mam says — so they sprinkle them for the sparrows instead.

On the way home, Da points out a large house with six chimneys and trees in the garden and tells Mam that one day they'll live in it.

When I come back for good your Uncle Frank and I are going into business, he says. We've got big plans, we have. I'll buy you a fur coat and a diamond ring. How would you like that?

Mam smiles and shakes her head, holding out her hand. That gold ring's enough for me, she says. Just you come home, Jack, that's all I want.

Then Alice has to go and sleep at Gran's house. She doesn't understand

133

why and is naughty, kicking and screaming when Uncle Frank comes to collect her. Uncle Frank finds a whole cake of Fry's chocolate cream in her coat pocket and tells her to be a good girl and give Da and Mam a couple of days on their own. Perhaps she could paint a picture for Da to take with him when he goes away.

The picture is on the back of an old piece of wallpaper and used up most of her paints. It's got Alice herself in it, holding hands with Mam and Da.

They all go, even Gran, to wave Da off at the station when he has to go back to the war. He shows Alice the special picture, rolled up carefully in his soldier's pack.

A few months later Mam stops working at the factory and starts crying a lot.

'How will we manage?' she asks Gran over and over, but for once Gran has nothing to say. She keeps on knitting something small and white.

Alice spends Christmas Eve with Gran that year and has a tangerine, a whole packet of barley sugar and a threepenny bit in the sock Uncle Frank hung up for her by the fire. At breakfast Gran gives her a hat and mittens, knitted in navy-blue wool she's unravelled from an old jumper. Uncle Frank gives her a new paint box.

But the best present comes later when Uncle Frank takes her home. A lady Alice has never seen before meets them at the door. She's wearing a white apron.

You must be Alice, she smiles. Come and see your mam. She has a surprise for you.

She leads Alice through to the bedroom where Mam is sitting up in bed and in her arms is a baby wrapped in a shawl. Mam draws the shawl back to show a little face, rather red and scrunched up. Alice isn't sure what to make of it.

Then the baby opens his eyes and appears to look right at her and straightaway Alice knows that she loves him more than anyone else in the whole wide world.

'Say hello to your baby brother,' Mam says. 'His name's Charlie.'

7

Stella almost danced up the stairs and into the flat some hours later, holding a warm, fragrant parcel. Celebratory fish and chips. She enjoyed them more than anything she'd eaten in a long time. And there were no marauding seagulls diving at the chips like that time in Berwick-upon-Tweed. She ate every single one.

'Alice was awake,' she told Isabel when she got back from her work night out. 'Dopey, not quite with it, but she was coherent, knew who I was. It's such a relief!'

'That's wonderful,' Isabel said.

'She asked after Maddie. I said she was fine but Alice didn't say any more and I didn't think she was up to any questions. I don't know if she remembered that Maddie was in Australia or not.' Stella sat down next to Isabel on the sofa. 'So please, Isabel, tell me what's going on. Who is Charlie?'

Isabel took a deep breath. 'Charlie is Alice's brother.'

'Alice's *brother*? *Alice's* brother? But she doesn't have one.'

'Well, Maddie said she had, that she has, I

mean. She has a long-lost brother called Charlie and he lives in Australia.'

Isabel made this sound as if it were something completely normal. But then she was used to dealing with customers, maybe some of them difficult, and, in her role as a first aider, with people who were upset in various ways. And Stella was upset. It still didn't make sense.

'Why have we never met him before?' she wondered aloud. Had there been a family quarrel? What would he be to Maddie and herself? Their great-uncle? For someone who'd never known any blood relatives except her sister, parents and granny it was too much to take in. 'I'm going to wake up in a minute back in London.' Stella put her head in her hands. 'This is like some bizarre dream.'

'Alice will explain everything I'm sure, when she's able to,' said Isabel soothingly. 'I wish I could tell you more. Actually, I haven't seen much of Maddie these last couple of weeks; I've been out a lot and she was staying late in the workshop with last-minute Christmas orders. But I'm looking forward to hearing all about it too. It sounds like it's quite a story.' She yawned and stood up. 'Time for bed. By the way, talking of Christmas, what are you going to do? You

137

won't be here on your own, will you? You're welcome to come with me to my mum and dad's. Christmas down on the farm.'

'Oh, that's lovely of you,' Stella said. As she had with Skye earlier she tried to sound chirpy when she replied, as if she were going to be spending the day in a normal happy way. 'But I'll have as much time as I can with Alice. Eat too much chocolate. Watch Christmas movies. The usual things.'

'The offer stands if you change your mind,' Isabel said, not sounding at all convinced.

* * *

Since he stopped playing for the county rugby team and for Scotland and after his broken shoulder had healed, Ross had started running. He'd seen other ex-players get out of shape when their competitive days were over, plus he had the temptations of the deli and the restaurant constantly in front of him. So several mornings a week he ran for an hour in the hills above the town. As well as the physical exercise he found it cleared his head.

But not today. He thought he'd got over the shock he'd felt the night of Gav and Carol's wedding when Stella told him that she was moving to London. Only for two years, she kept repeating, but she might as well have said it was forever. She was very good at her job, he knew that, and part of him was very proud of her, but mostly he was shattered to know that she'd decided to go without discussing it with him, and wouldn't listen to his desperate attempts to accommodate that decision. He started to say he would go too — frantically, he began to think through the details. But she'd said that wouldn't work and they'd ended up shouting at each other.

Now he knew that the hurt of that moment was still there. Seeing her again brought it right into the open. Try as he might, as he ran along the path below Mid Hill, he couldn't forget it.

Even coming up onto the hill reminded him of Stella, all the fun they'd had up here with Gav and the gang, little Maddie trailing behind calling 'Wait for me!' At ten or eleven he and Stella had a special friendship, their own imaginary games about Roman legions and Border reivers and Thomas the Rhymer, fuelled by the tales his grandpa and her granny had told them.

Later, in their teens and early twenties, they didn't see so much of each other, except when they both happened to be home in Melrose at the same time. Rugby. Different universities. Different friends. Relationships. And then that Christmas Eve party of Bette's when they suddenly looked at each other with new eyes.

He increased his pace over the cold hard ground. It was pointless to think of that. But sitting opposite her in the café yesterday had brought it all back, like a film playing on an endless loop in his head.

With lungs at bursting point he came to a stop and bent over, panting, catching his breath. Standing up, he found he was above Hill View.

He would go and see Lilias now. Get it over with, he thought, rather ashamedly. It wasn't as if he minded helping a neighbour, of course he didn't. It was a natural thing to do, growing up as he had with a grandfather like Gray and a mother like Bette, ready to volunteer themselves for anything, in a community where everybody knew each other. But it was hard to get away from Lilias. He couldn't pop in for only a few minutes to fire up the range. She followed him around finding other little jobs for him to do, to detain him so that she needn't be on her own. Talking endlessly, almost to herself. Talking about Alice. Talking about Stella. What a lovely girl she was. Pretty and so clever. Wouldn't it be nice if she and Ross could be boyfriend and girlfriend again? Alice would be so pleased . . .

But the poor soul was worried about being in charge of the house — that wasn't supposed to happen — and lonely by herself. When Alice was able to have visitors he and Mum could take her up to the Infirmary.

Today, Lilias pointed out a large area of damp she'd found in the kitchen cupboard. There was a mouse caught in a trap to be disposed of, a light bulb to change, and wood to chop to feed that blessed range. Lilias pattered behind him, murmuring about how many eggs the hens had laid, and how she brushed dear Patch's coat yesterday and . . .

Ross refused the offer of tea but accepted a glass of water. He was sitting at the table drinking it when the phone rang.

Lilias carried on chatting. 'And I said to Patch — '

'Aren't you going to answer that?' Ross interrupted.

'Oh no, dear. I never answer the phone. I don't like it. It might be bad news.'

'But what if it's about . . . shall I get it?' He went into the hall. 'Hello. Hill View.'

'Who's that? Ross? Where's Lilias?'

Stella.

'She's here, well, in the kitchen. Doesn't do

phones, apparently.' Ross raised his eyebrows questioningly although there was no one there to see him.

'Doesn't do phones? Maddie's been ringing, hoping of course to speak to Alice. Why does Lilias not pick up?'

'Your guess is as good as mine. But how do you know, about Maddie, I mean?' Could it be that they were having an everyday, friendly conversation?

'She emailed Gray — he read it out to me. Did he say anything to you?'

'I haven't seen him today yet.'

'Will he be at home now?'

'I would think so. Oh, by the way, if you're making a list, of things to be done here I mean, you've got a damp problem too, in that big kitchen cupboard.'

'What?' Suddenly it wasn't a friendly conversation any more. 'Please don't tell me any more faults you find. It's . . . it's not helpful.'

'I — '

She'd hung up. Fine. Well, he wouldn't be helpful. What was the point?

'That was Stella,' he told Lilias, realising as he opened his mouth that he hadn't asked after Alice.

★ ★ ★

142

'Gray? It's Stella.'

'How are things?' His voice was wary, prepared to hear unwelcome news.

'Much improved. Alice spoke to me when I went in last night — not much but it's a start. And she had a good night's sleep, the nurse said this morning.'

'That's such a relief.' Gray sounded quite overcome. 'And she'll make a full recovery?'

'They won't commit themselves but it's looking positive. Gray, thanks for telling me about Maddie's email.'

'Yes, good to know she got there safely.' Clearly Gray was trying to concentrate on that aspect of Maddie's communication but Stella wasn't going to let the rest of it pass.

'I didn't know Alice had a brother, Gray! Why am I the last to know? Isabel told me last night, at least that there was a brother called Charlie, she didn't know anything else.'

'I should have told you that myself,' Gray said. 'But it's a big thing, isn't it? The story would come so much better from Alice. She hasn't told me everything — it's brought back a lot of raw memories I think. I understand that they were separated when they were very little children.'

'That's terrible. Poor Granny. But how did she find him?'

'He found her. I suppose it's much easier

to access official records and so on these days. She got a letter from him completely out of the blue.'

Tears came into Stella's eyes. 'I hope I'll be able to tell her soon that Maddie's met him and says he's lovely.' She felt in her pocket for a tissue. 'So really and truly you never knew about him before?'

She sensed Gray shaking his head before he replied, 'No, I've known Alice for almost fifty years, ever since she married your grandfather and came to live here. There was an uncle I think that she was fond of but he'd died a few years before. She never said much about her parents and nothing about a brother.'

'I suppose he is her brother? Not someone else who thinks she's a soft touch.'

'Hardly likely, my dear. Not all the way from Australia. I daresay we shall find out all about it when Alice is well enough to tell us. Now, when are we going to see you again?'

'I'm not sure. I'll let you know when Alice can have other visitors.'

'Good,' said Gray. 'Skye's down here as you probably know. But you'll have Maddie's other flatmate for company, won't you? And of course you'll be with us for Christmas.' It wasn't a question.

'I don't know about that, Gray. I'm not sure what I'm going to do.' *But it certainly*

144

won't be spending Christmas in Melrose.
'Love to Bette,' she said quickly, before he could respond. 'I'll be in touch.'

'Look forward to that and, oh, don't worry about Lilias and the house. We'll keep an eye on them. Take care, sweetheart.'

'Lilias! I never told Ross — ' But Gray had gone.

★   ★   ★

The flat was empty. As Gray had reminded her, Skye was in Melrose, and Isabel had left to go to work.

For something to do she found a vacuum cleaner and did the hall and Maddie's room, getting rid of large fluff balls from under the bed. Maddie wouldn't mind — at least she'd never minded anyone tidying up after her before.

Also under the bed were boxes of jewellery. Earrings in one. Bracelets. Necklaces. Each piece had a little label attached: *Maddie Makes*. One caught Stella's eye and she lifted it out. Three little charms, a black Scottie dog, a red-and-white-spotted bow and an ivory-coloured bone, were threaded onto a piece of thin ribbon. It was unusual and very effective. She examined the others; they were equally quirky and charming. Clever old

Maddie. Isabel was right. She had got serious about her work.

Even though she felt less than festive she could go up to Princes Street and see the Christmas sights, look at the shops. She had bought presents in London for Alice and Maddie but she should get a little gift for Isabel, and for Skye too, and some food for herself. And she must get Alice some new nightclothes.

She made a cup of coffee and sat down to make a list of things but found herself writing *Charlie??* She frowned as she tried to recollect what she knew about her grandmother's early life. Alice never talked about it much, she realised now. Her family came from a town somewhere in the north of England. She had an Uncle Frank who taught her how to paint when she was very small, she'd told her granddaughters. He could do anything with his hands, Uncle Frank could. Make or mend anything. When he died he left her just enough money to fund her going to art college, and she'd named the girls' father after him. Very occasionally Alice would mention 'Gran' or 'Mam' or 'my father' — but never 'Charlie' or 'my brother'.

Why had Stella not been interested enough to ask questions about Alice's family — her own family too, after all? It was as if Alice had hardly existed until she went to study art in

Edinburgh and met John Greenlaw in her last year there, literally bumping into him one day in a gallery. She loved to tell her granddaughters about that romantic meeting.

But Charlie existed even though Alice never spoke of him.

Stella picked up her phone. Google knew practically everything, didn't it? The answer to any question at the touch of a few buttons. What was Alice's maiden name? Something short. Dodds. Alice Dodds.

She typed in 'Charlie Dodds'. Nothing likely came up. She added 'Coolharbour Australia' and waited to find her long-lost great-uncle. Nothing. If there was anyone called Charlie Dodds in Coolharbour he had done nothing to bring himself to the attention of the world wide web.

She put the place name in on its own. A small town south of Sydney, as Pete had said, 'renowned for the number of artists and craft workers who live there'. It looked as though Charlie had the artistic gene too. But how had he ended up so far away, out of touch with his own family?

When she clicked on 'images' Coolharbour sprang into view. It was a quaint little place, with narrow streets leading down to the eponymous harbour. How odd to think that Maddie was there, getting to know it and

Charlie and his family. His family! That meant they had cousins too — whether second cousins, or cousins once or twice removed she wasn't sure how to work out. It wasn't a subject that had ever cropped up in her life before.

Her phone rang, startling her away from the subject of faraway relatives to one close to home. The hospital. 'Yes?' She waited with dread to hear what they had to say. Surely they wouldn't contact her if everything was fine.

It was a different nurse this time. 'Your grandmother's become a little agitated and the doctor says it would probably help if you could speak to her. She's actually asking for someone called Charlie but we have no contact details for that name. Do you know him?'

There wasn't an easy answer to that question. 'He lives abroad. Shall I come in now?'

'Yes. Come to the nursing bay first.'

Forty-five minutes later the nurse led her to Alice's room. 'Here's your granddaughter, Alice. Here's Stella come to see you.'

Alice lay with her top half slightly elevated. Her hands clutched the bedcover and her eyes darted over to the door. 'Is Charlie with you? Is Charlie coming?'

Stella sat down and took Alice's hands between her own.

'Charlie is in Australia. Do you remember that Maddie's gone out to see him? She arrived safely and she says Charlie is well and happy.' Not strictly true perhaps but surely 'brilliant' implied that.

'Well and happy.' Alice focused her eyes on Stella as she repeated her words. 'Well and happy.' Her face relaxed with relief.

'Why . . . ' Stella started to ask. Why didn't you tell us about Charlie? What happened in your family? And why did Maddie go out to Australia? But all these and a thousand more questions were going to have to wait until Alice was strong enough to answer them.

'The place Charlie lives in, Coolharbour; it's lovely. I looked it up online,' she said instead. 'Down from Sydney, on the coast. Full of painters and glassmakers and silversmiths and people doing all manner of different things. Maddie will love it.' She wondered about getting out her phone to show her granny the images but Alice was murmuring something she didn't catch.

She leaned in closer. 'What did you say, darling?'

'Did I fall?'

'Yes. You were on a ladder trying to hang a picture.'

Alice tried to nod. 'Lilias's picture. What day was that? I was going to phone you.'

'That was Monday. It's Thursday now.'

'It had to be Maddie.' Alice sounded drowsy. 'Sorry to be such a nuisance.'

Stella rubbed her grandmother's hands gently. 'Ssh. Don't say that.'

Alice was right about one thing though. There would have been no question of Stella going to Coolharbour even if she'd been told about Charlie. Her one experience of flying, on a school trip to France, had ended in tears — she'd never been in an aeroplane since, never wanted to. A legacy from the childhood memory of hearing how her parents died was how she'd diagnosed it herself.

But Maddie's so trusting, she thought. It should have been me going out to see this Charlie. Who knew what sort of person he might have turned into? Maddie would be seeing the situation through rosy spectacles, loving the drama and adventure of it all.

'You look worried, snooky-pie.' The childhood endearment brought tears to Stella's eyes. 'You were always such a worrier.' Alice's eyes flickered. 'Well and happy. My baby brother. Sleep now.'

Stella stayed until Alice's grip slackened. 'She calmed down and now she's sleeping,' she said to the nurse. 'I'll come back tonight.

When can she have other visitors?'

'Let's see. Today's Thursday. If all goes well, I would say Saturday. Not a crowd, mind. One at a time.'

8

Alice walks on tiptoes holding on to the handlebar of Charlie's pram. She nudges Mam's hand away so that she's pushing it all by herself up Gran's path. Charlie is six months old and he can sit up. If she stretches her neck Alice can just see him, his cheeks round and red because his teeth are coming through.

Mam is back at the factory and now Gran looks after Alice and Charlie.

I'm getting too old for this lark, Gran says, a bit grumbly sounding. But she cuddles Charlie and Alice fetches nappies or Charlie's bottle or a teething ring and shows him her latest picture but from a distance in case he grabs it and stuffs it into his mouth.

Uncle Frank has got a camera called a box brownie. He gets Alice to sit on the floor holding Charlie. He says 'watch the birdie' and he snaps the shutter. Next time he comes round he has the photographs on shiny paper. In the one Alice likes best, Charlie is looking up at her as if she's his favourite person in the whole wide world. He holds an end of her long hair very firmly in his fat little fist.

Charlie is a year old. He wants to crawl and he wriggles to get down from Gran's lap. He wears out the knees of his knitted trousers scooting about the house.

He begins to walk. Alice does less painting and more running after him to stop him getting into mischief. She doesn't always manage it. Charlie falls down the back step and cuts his forehead. He stalks Gran's cat until it gets fed up and goes to live next door.

Alice is very proud that Charlie's first word is 'Ally'. That's what it sounds like anyway. She is Big Sister Ally. She begins to tell him all the stories that Uncle Frank has told her. Charlie seems to listen, grinning, showing four pearly teeth, two up and two down. When they go out, Charlie staggers between Uncle Frank and Alice, holding onto each of them tightly. It takes a very long time to walk round the corner.

Charlie is almost two when Da comes back from the war.

Da doesn't come to live with them. He lives in a place called a home but it's not with Mam and Alice and Charlie. Mam goes to see him on her days off. Sometimes she takes Charlie with her.

Once Uncle Frank takes Alice up to the home. They don't go inside but they see Da through a window. He's sitting in a chair with wheels attached. He's looking at them, so Alice waves her hand. He doesn't wave back.

Will Da always live there? Alice asks, and Uncle Frank says, I won't tell you a lie, Alice. Yes, I'm sorry to say he will.

The munitions factory closes down and Mam doesn't go out to work any more. She sits in the house and cries, or walks for hours pushing Charlie in his pram. Alice is a big girl of five and has started going to school. The teacher pins all of Alice's paintings on the wall and brings other teachers in to see them. Uncle Frank takes her to school in the morning and waits at the gate for her at half-past three.

One day they walk home, Alice swinging as she always does on Uncle Frank's hand. Usually he tells her, in a pretend scary voice, not to step on the pavement cracks or the bogie man will get her. Or he has a new joke for her, or a funny little rhyme. But today he's quiet, walking along with his head down. She wonders if he has a sore tummy from eating too much of Gran's dumpling. Uncle Frank is very fond of dumpling.

There's something else strange. Usually when they go into the hall even Alice has to make herself thin to get past the pram. But today it isn't there. Mam hasn't taken Charlie out because she's lying on the sofa all curled up. Charlie isn't with her. He isn't in bed. He isn't anywhere.

Charlie has gone.

9

'Hi there.'

'Skye. Good to see you.' Ross came round to the front of the deli counter. 'I really appreciate you helping us out.'

'Better wait until tomorrow evening to say thank you,' Skye laughed, reaching up to kiss his cheek. 'I hope your excellent reputation will still be intact.'

Ross wouldn't tell her that Tom had said more or less the same thing.

'I'm not worried,' he said.

Skye was petite and very pretty in a quilted jacket, her fair curls spilling out from under a pink woolly hat. She took the hat off and shook her head so that the curls sprang back into place.

'I've got my cap and my chef's whites with me,' she said. 'Lucky I kept them or I'd have to borrow from Tom.'

Ross thought of his burly chef, his girth evidence of his love of food. 'I don't think that would have worked, do you?'

She put her hand on his arm. 'You and I could probably both get into them.'

He took a step back.

'I wasn't going to pounce on you.' Skye grinned at him. 'I'm in professional mode today. Besides, I was speaking to Stella and — '

'And what?'

'When you told her I was coming down here, did you tell her I was cooking? I don't think I actually said that? Anyway, she was like a deer in the headlights. Stricken.'

Ross went to call through the connecting door. 'Tom! Skye's here.' He turned back. 'Your name didn't come up,' he said. 'What I do or who I see is nothing to do with her.'

'If you say so,' said Skye, taking off her jacket.

'You and Tom can sit here to go through the menu and I'll throw in my two penceworth if necessary.' He indicated the table in the window. 'This is going to be my mini café when the coffee machine is delivered in the New Year. Ah, here's Tom now,' he said, thankful to have a third party in the room. 'You remember Skye, Tom? She enjoyed your dinner here a few months ago.'

Well, that was clever, reminding Skye of that evening.

'She'll have to cook something for me tonight and see if I enjoy it!' Tom said, shaking Skye's hand heartily.

'I'll leave you to it,' Ross said, as the bell

indicated he had a customer. He was pleased to see that it was Carol, Gav's wife.

'Rossie! How are you? I've only got a minute. Gav's sister says you've got a brilliant venison pâté — I thought it would make an easy starter on Christmas Day. What'll I need — a couple of those big tubs?'

'How many are you feeding?'

She ticked them off on her fingers. 'My mum. Me. Gav. His sister and brother-in-law. Their three kids. Although they'll hate it. I'll get them something else. Some of your smoked salmon. And give me two lots of pâté anyway — maybe we'll have unexpected guests.' She gave him one of her looks, as if he should be able to tell what she was thinking. 'And,' she rattled on, as he rang up her purchases, 'I was wondering if you'd like to come round to ours tomorrow night, have a bite to eat, catch up?'

'Are you kidding?' He grinned at her. 'Two days before Christmas? It'll be a madhouse here.'

'That's what Gav said but I wanted to ask you something. We're having the babe christened the week after New Year, the Sunday, and it would be great to have a lunch party here at Uncle Ross's restaurant afterwards.'

'Oh, well, if you're putting business my

way,' Ross teased. 'It would be good to catch up with you both. No chance of tomorrow evening, though, Carol. I could pop up for an hour during the day if that suits you.'

'Twoish, threeish suit you? I'm going to Edinburgh with Mum. I'll text you.' She blew him a kiss as she left.

He must remember to ask Bette if the baby was a boy or a girl. Since it must be about two months old it was rather late in the day to ask Gav's sister to remind him, and he could hardly refer to the child as 'it' tomorrow.

He hoped that Gav would be there too — they hadn't seen each other properly for ages, plus he had a calming effect on Carol. If she let him get a word in edgeways.

The received wisdom was that opposites attract, but it was true too that some couples looked almost as if they could be brother and sister. Did they start out that way or did they change over the years?

The 'opposites attract' theory wasn't only about physical appearance of course but about personality, interests, outlook. Gav thought before he spoke and hid his dry sense of humour until he knew someone really well, while Carol fizzed with life and could talk for Scotland — what you saw was what you got with Carol right from the start. How would their baby turn out? Ross wondered. Which parent would it take after or would it be a combination of the two of them?

He wasn't sure if he liked being called 'Uncle Ross' — it was sweet in one way but positively elderly in another . . .

'Ross.' Tom beckoned to him. 'We've been through the menus. See what you think.'

'I trust you but let's have a look.' He pulled up a chair.

'Skye says she makes a mean risotto,' Tom said, 'so we've put that as the veggie option at lunchtime.'

Ross read down the menus quickly. It all sounded delicious. Apart from the mushroom risotto. But that was just him. He was sure the customers would love it. 'Terrific.' He nodded at Tom. 'You could find yourself out of a job.'

'No chance,' said Skye. 'I'm looking forward to this but I prefer to set my own hours, thank you. I'm afraid I didn't have what it took to work all hours, every day. I couldn't stand the heat so I got out of the kitchen.'

'It's not easy,' Tom agreed. 'But I can't imagine doing anything else.'

'Although funnily enough, I love staying really late at the workshop when I've got an order to finish. It gives me a real buzz.'

Tom waggled his eyebrows up and down.

'This is a pretty buzzy place, isn't it, Ross?'

Ross didn't rise to Tom's banter. 'I'll catch up with you later,' he said to Skye. 'Tom will show you the kitchen now.'

'Yes, boss.' Tom gave a mock salute and was about to escort Skye through the back of the deli when Bette came in.

Bad timing. Bette had guessed that he'd spent a night with Skye — she'd enquired after Maddie and then put two and two together. She made no comment — why should she? He was a free agent. But he suspected she wasn't happy about it because of Skye and Maddie being friends.

'Mum, you remember Skye?' he said, trying to sound nonchalant. 'She came to stay with Maddie one weekend.'

His mother didn't let him down. 'Yes, of course.' She smiled politely at Skye. 'You brought Alice that lovely jug you made. She was thrilled with it.'

'I'm sorry about her accident,' Skye said.

'My father and I are hoping we'll be able to visit her soon. Ross, do you have time for a quick word?'

'Of course. Tom, Skye, I'll see you later. Skye, I'm doing front-of-house tonight. Everything all right, Mum?'

'Fine,' Bette said. 'Just to remind you that I'll be out all day tomorrow.' She was going to pick up Kenneth, Ross's dad, from Glasgow Airport early in the morning. They had to see a solicitor to finalise the purchase of their new house and then would visit relatives of Kenneth's before coming home. 'Will you have time to pop in and see your grandpa?'

'Of course. Is he all right?'

'He's been very down since Alice's accident. He won't admit it but I can tell. They've been such good friends all these years. There's hardly been a day when they haven't chewed the fat, put the world to rights. He's missing her.'

'I'll go after lunch. Then I'm nipping up to see Gav and Carol — they want to have the christening party here. Oh, Mum, I've forgotten, did they have a boy or a girl?'

'Men.' Bette shook her head. 'It's a little girl. Emily.'

'Emily, Emily. Right, I've got that. Hope all goes well tomorrow — oh, but I'll see you later. I'll sleep at yours tonight and tomorrow if that's okay — Skye will be in the flat.'

'I see.' Bette's face gave no indication of her thoughts. 'Of course you can.' She made no move to go. 'Have you . . . have you heard anything from Stella?'

'Why should I have?'

'It's a hard time for her. Alice is everything to those girls. It's at a time like this that Stella must feel the lack of other relatives.'

'I suppose so. I didn't think of it like that.' Ross thought of his own family. Bette was an only child but on his father's side there was a host of uncles and aunts and cousins. 'But what can I do? We're barely on speaking terms — and that was her idea, remember?'

'I know,' Bette sighed. 'I'll never understand why she did what she did, taking off to London like that.'

'Yes, well.' Ross didn't want to have yet another variation of this conversation. 'What's done is done. Excuse me, Mum. I've a pile of things to do.'

'Sorry, darling.' Bette stretched up to give him a quick hug. 'See you later.'

Back behind the counter, Ross picked up his phone. What could he say in a text message to Stella that would be supportive but not friendly? It was too much of an ask.

Especially as he'd deleted her from his contacts list.

★   ★   ★

Stella got off the number twenty-four bus. It was late morning, three days before Christmas, and Princes Street bustled with shoppers. The German market beside the Royal Scottish Academy was so busy she could hardly walk through it so she retreated back onto the street.

On her right-hand side a train glided into Waverley Station. Down in Princes Street Gardens water had been flooded in and frozen to make a skating rink and it was busy both with competent skaters and people holding on to each other, laughing if they fell over. That was a comic Christmas-card scene — but the wider picture showed the dull winter green of the gardens; stalls selling food and mulled wine; the wheel — Edinburgh's equivalent of the London Eye over the Christmas period; the towering monument to one of Scotland's greatest, if now largely unread, writers; and behind that, but from this angle almost appearing to be part of it, that brightly coloured fairground ride that moved up and down as well as whizzed round and round. A more-than-life-size statue of Sir Walter Scott sat in the middle of his monument, stonily unaware of the gaiety going on around him. But none of these attractions were much fun if you were on your own.

She crossed the road and went up to the lingerie department of Marks & Spencer's to choose nightwear for Alice. It was full of men, presumably doing last-minute Christmas shopping. She exited the shop as soon as she'd made her purchases and walked round to Hanover Street, where it was a little quieter. A coffee would be good before she faced the crowded shops again.

Grand old buildings, modern office blocks, tenement flats, all huddled together. Edinburgh was a city that had grown organically over many centuries. She knew it well but it could still surprise her. She'd forgotten how breathtaking the view was from further down Hanover Street when the road sloped away and you found yourself looking right over the city to the Firth of Forth, and beyond to the coast of Fife.

Brrr! It was cold, much colder than in London. The downside of that view was the wind whistling off the water and up the street. She didn't remember it bothering her before. The last fifteen months in the south must have softened her. But it was lovely to be back, despite the circumstances, and for the moment to have no one to please but herself. To wander down this street with its cafés — many more since she'd last been here — and its small art galleries . . .

She stopped in her tracks. The painting displayed in the front of the Lothian Gallery's window looked to be very much in the style of the oil Lilias had given to Alice. A seascape this time, in blues and greys — who knew there were so many different tones of these two colours? A boat on the horizon disappeared the closer Stella got to it.

This couldn't be by Lilias, could it? Was there a signature? Yes, but it was difficult to make out. The surname might begin with Av. She didn't know if she'd ever heard what Lilias's second name was. The first initial could be an L but was equally likely to be I.

The gallery's location suggested prestige and high prices. Stella peered inside, caught someone's eye. Should she go in or not? She looked at the seascape again, and thought of the painting hanging in Alice's hall. Yes, she would swear they were by the same person. There was one way to find out.

'The Irene Avery? We've only recently acquired it. I shouldn't think we'll have it for long. She's much sought after but, sadly, not very prolific.' The assistant was a smooth-talking young man. How could you tell if what he said was true or a sales pitch?

'What can you tell me about her?'

He reached for a sheet of paper and handed it over. 'We don't know a lot, unfortunately. That's about it.'

'Can I keep this?' Stella asked, not wanting to read it in front of him.

'Of course.'

'And can I ask the price of the painting?' His eyes lit up. 'It's on there as well.'

Stella unfolded the sheet she was about to put in her bag. She couldn't help gasping. 'Fifteen thousand pounds!'

'Beautiful to have on your wall, and a sound investment, I can promise you.'

'Well, thank you for your help. I can't buy it but I agree it's beautiful. I'm sure, as you say, that you won't have it long.'

'I can take it out of the window so you can see it better,' the young man persisted.

Luckily the door was pushed open at that moment to announce a well-heeled couple and Stella made her escape. Perhaps they would be the new owners of the painting by Irene Avery, whoever she was.

She ducked into the nearest café, ordered a latte, and sat down to see if the information on the paper provided any clues.

Irene Lilias Avery was born in London in 1943 and entered the Royal College of Art in 1962. She left the RCA without finishing her degree. Nevertheless, she had several successful exhibitions in London before moving, with her sister, to live quietly in the south of Scotland. Her first exhibition in many years, in Edinburgh in 2015, was a sell-out. Her early work has been reappraised and now commands high prices.

There followed a string of review quotes: *Stunning . . . traditionally modern . . . where have you been, Irene? . . . everyone wants an Avery.*

Stella felt stunned herself.

Why was Lilias — because it was undoubtedly her — living with Alice as if she didn't have two pennies to rub together? And what happened after that promising start to her career?

She wrapped her hands round the warm cup. Gray might be able to throw some light on the matter — and she could tell him about the unexpected visit to the Infirmary she'd made after she'd spoken to him this morning.

Huddling into the corner of the café she tried to speak on her phone at a level that he could hear but that wouldn't disturb the other customers. Gray was happy to know that he should be able to visit his old friend soon and promised that he would walk round to tell Lilias that Alice was improving.

'Talking of Lilias, Gray, I'm in Hanover Street and I've seen a painting of hers in a gallery,' Stella said. 'Did you know she's very well thought of?' Shamefacedly, she recalled her quick dismissal of Gray's high opinion of Lilias's work the other day in the car, and her own subsequent amazement when she saw an example for herself in Hill View.

'Yes, there was quite a bit of publicity about her last year when she had an exhibition,' Gray said. 'An interesting character. Problems with her nerves most of her life, I believe. Or at least that's what they used to call it. Shame. Probably could have been helped if she was born later. But such talent.'

'How come she's ended up staying with Alice?'

'Lived with her younger sister, bossed about by her by all accounts. Then at the ripe old age of sixty-five the sister upped and got married. Lilias had never lived by herself. Didn't know what to do. Alice heard about her and, well, you know your granny.'

'I do know,' said Stella.

'She not only asked Lilias to come and stay with her but persuaded her to start painting again, and rang around the galleries, persisting until she got someone to come down here. Lilias was offered an exhibition on the spot.'

'Quite a story. I love her Hill View painting, although it did cause Alice to end up in hospital.'

Stella became aware that the woman at the next table had paused, a piece of millionaire shortbread halfway to her mouth, obviously listening to the conversation.

'Gray, I'm in a café. I better go.'

'Hold on, Stella. You're the second Greenlaw sister I've heard from today. Maddie phoned me after you did this morning.'

'Maddie phoned!' She was speaking too loudly. Now other people were turning in her direction, torn between disapproval and nosiness. 'Gray, I can't talk now. How is she?'

'Great. But wondering of course why she's not been able to speak to Alice.'

'She must be worried sick. I'll call you right back.'

She gulped down the remainder of her coffee. Back in Hanover Street she found a doorway to a shop that was shut for refurbishment and scrolled for Gray's home number. He must have been waiting by the phone.

'I had to tell her, Stella. I hope I did the right thing. Not the whole story. Just that Alice had hurt her ankle falling off a ladder and was in hospital in Edinburgh.'

'Yes — it's true as far as it goes anyway. But what else did she say? What's she doing?'

'Having a whale of a time by the sound of it. Most of Charlie's family are artists one way or another. Maddie's in her element,' Gray laughed.

'But does she know why he and Alice lost contact?' It was lovely that Maddie was happy

170

but there were questions that had to be asked.

'You know, I'm not sure that he knows very much himself — he wasn't much more than a baby apparently when he was adopted.'

'Adopted? That's so sad. I wonder what happened, what Alice will remember? But she would have been very little herself.' All those years of separation. 'I can see why it would be too painful for her to think about, never mind talk about.'

'Indeed,' said Gray. 'So Maddie knows now that Alice had her accident before she could tell you about it. Hold on, I'll give you the number — it's Charlie's landline.'

Stella put her handbag on the ground so she could have both hands free, and alternately listened to Gray and punched in the numbers.

'It'll be night in Sydney, won't it?' she asked. 'Do you know what time?'

'Not sure — ten, eleven o'clock? Maybe later.'

'Is it too late to call?'

'Up to you, sweetheart. I think it's time you and Maddie talked. You can reassure her about Alice and maybe get a message from Charlie to pass on to her.'

Stella gathered up the lapels of her jacket and held them to her neck. 'I wish I was in Sydney — it's freezing here! Yes, I'll call her now. And if Alice can have visitors you'll come up on Christmas Eve?'

'You bet. Do you think I should take Lilias?'

'Maybe wait a bit longer for that. Until Alice is well enough to cope with her. She's quite hard work. It would be great if Bette could come though — she's always so practical.'

'And you'll come back down with us, for Christmas?'

'I don't know, Gray.' *No. No. No.* 'I'll ring Maddie now. I'll be in touch.'

Eagerly she keyed in the number. There was so much to say even if it couldn't all be said while standing in a draughty doorway. She'd repeat what Gray had told Maddie about Alice, not mentioning that she'd been knocked out; she'd say she was staying in Maddie's room and then she'd hear all about their great-uncle and his family. She could almost hear Maddie's excitement as she waited.

'Charlie Hollis.' Hollis. So that's why she couldn't find him on the web. It was him — Alice's long-lost brother.

'Hello, this is Stella. Maddie's sister. Alice's granddaughter.'

'Stella! That's made my day. Are you as terrific as your sister? We love her! And Alice

172

— she's in hospital? That's not good.'

'She's doing well,' Stella said, mentally crossing her fingers. How dreadful it would have been if she'd had to give Charlie bad news. 'I'll see her tonight. I can't tell you how thrilled she'll be to know I've spoken to you.'

'You give her a big hug from me, Stella, and one for yourself. Maddie's right here.'

Maddie wanted to know how Alice had fallen and how she was, and she was frustrated that she couldn't speak to her.

'You came home when you heard about it?'

'I'm in Edinburgh, staying in your room. Well, at the moment I'm standing in Hanover Street in a howling gale.'

'I'm standing in Charlie's hall. I can see yellow sand and blue sea. Blue-green sea. It's beautiful. We're going to have Christmas on the beach.'

'Lucky old you! So, they're nice, are they?'

'Fantastic. Imagine us having cousins and an auntie and everything!' And she was off, sounding as excited as Stella had imagined. The names of Charlie's wife and daughters and grandchildren, even a great-grandchild. The shops, the crafts, in Coolharbour. The endless sunshine. Eventually she ran out of breath.

'Sorry Stell, this call must be costing you a fortune. I've got a phone now — Briony helped me choose.' Before Stella had a chance to ask how Briony fitted into the family, Maddie gave Stella her new number and asked, 'Will Alice get out of hospital for Christmas?'

'I don't think so.' Oops. Maddie would be suspicious — surely a broken ankle wouldn't merit being in for another few days. 'Mads, it's great to hear you. I think I'm about to run out of charge.' Which was true. 'We'll speak soon.'

Isabel kicked off her shoes and swung her legs onto the sofa. 'I hate Thursdays. Especially the Thursday before Christmas. Late-night shopping night. Two days to go! Two days to go! Not sure my tootsies want to believe that though. They're ready to go home for Christmas right now.'

Stella laughed. 'It must be hard being on your feet all day. Guess what.' She picked up her phone and waved it at Isabel. 'I've got an app that will let me contact Maddie easily, and not use up all my battery.' She told Isabel about her conversation with Maddie — and Charlie. 'Hearing that I spoke to him was better than any medicine for Alice tonight.'

'It's just like that telly programme I catch sometimes,' Isabel said. 'Families get separated for all sorts of reasons. It's heartbreaking — I always have a box of tissues handy when I watch. But it's amazing the ways people can be traced. Alice must be sooo happy. How about a Chinese takeaway to celebrate?'

Stella thought about it.

'Why don't we go out? My treat.' Hang the expense, she thought. 'Is there somewhere nice nearby?'

'Ooh you don't have to do that, Stella.'

'I do,' said Stella. 'I really appreciate being able to stay here and you've been so nice.'

'There's a new Italian restaurant round the corner,' Isabel said. 'Skye and I had a pizza there when it opened. Great! I don't feel sleepy any more.'

Stella didn't want to talk about Skye. 'Right,' she said. She stood up and held out her hand to pull Isabel to her feet. 'Sounds good,' she said. 'I feel hungry just thinking about it.'

The street sparkled at night; in fact it looked better in the dark than during the day. Christmas trees shone out of most of the windows of the flats in the tenement buildings. Fairy lights. Baubles. Tinsel. Some a myriad of colours, some in tasteful themes.

At Hill View, the tree was always in the front hall, never put up until three evenings before Christmas. Alice made a party of the occasion, with homemade mince pies and star-shaped biscuits. When they'd been at primary school they asked friends, including Ross, round to join in the tree decorating.

Every year Alice and Maddie would contrive to make the tree slightly different in appearance from the year before, with decorations of their own making.

Then there were precious glass balls with nativity scenes inside that had been in their grandfather's family, carefully taken out every year and a thing of wonder to the girls when they were little.

The fairy was bought for them by Alice the first Christmas they were with her. They all had to make a wish, Alice said, but they mustn't tell anybody what it was. *I wish my mummy and daddy would come back.* That was Stella's first Christmas wish, maybe the second too. But after that the wishes were more easily granted. *I wish for a doll's pram. I wish Granny would let me walk to school on my own. I wish I'd pass my exams.* She didn't know about Maddie but she still silently spoke to the Christmas fairy as it was placed at the top of the tree.

Alice always bought the tree locally. Would it be delivered as usual? Stella suddenly wondered. She hated to think of it being dragged into the hall and left lying, undecorated, the fairy and the nativity baubles still wrapped in tissue paper in their special boxes in the dark cupboard under the stairs.

She was glad to sit down at the restaurant table. High heels and cobbled streets were not an ideal combination.

Warm garlicky smells came from the open kitchen where the chefs could be seen tossing pizza dough, and she felt herself relax into her comfortable chair.

Isabel leaned back too. 'Thanks for suggesting this,' she said. 'I can almost feel the Christmas break starting now. Two days to go!'

'Are you looking forward to going to your parents'?'

Isabel nodded. 'Bliss. Mum always makes me have breakfast in bed. And we're all going to my brother's for Christmas lunch. He's got two kids. It'll be fun.'

Stella felt a stab of envy. She missed the idea of having a mum and dad more than the reality because she hardly remembered her parents. There were photos of them of course and Alice told them stories about when their father was little but now Stella wondered what her and Maddie's lives would have been like if the accident hadn't happened, if they'd had a proper family. But that sounded so disloyal to Alice.

'Where do your parents live?' she asked,

realising she knew very little about her companion.

'On a farm near Stirling,' Isabel replied as she accepted a menu from the waitress.

Stella looked at her over her own menu. 'So you're a country girl too.'

'Born and bred. But a city girl now. It's great to know the farm's there, to go back to visit, but I love living here. There's so much to do in Edinburgh but it's small enough you can walk to most places. At home it's always a big expedition to get anywhere. And if you don't drive you're stuck.'

'You don't drive?'

'Sat my test four times. Failed my test four times,' Isabel said ruefully. 'I can drive. But I get beyond nervous when it comes to proving it.'

Stella was surprised. Isabel struck her as being so capable, as if she'd be able to do anything she put her mind to.

'So do you think of yourself as a country girl?' Isabel asked.

'I loved growing up in Melrose. I think about it so much when I'm in London. Don't get me wrong. There are lots of great things about it but . . . ' A bustling, crowded city, everyone minding their own business, can make one person feel very insignificant. But she wasn't going to burden Isabel any more with Stella Greenlaw's problems. She didn't finish the sentence. 'Let's see the menu. Their Christmas specials sound interesting.'

'Mmm. I think I'll have the mushroom risotto though. See if it's as good as Skye's.'

Ross hated mushrooms, Stella remembered, not without satisfaction. So Skye wouldn't find the way to his heart through that dish.

'Pumpkin gnocchi,' Stella said to the waitress. 'And a glass of house white.'

'Red for me,' Isabel said, giving her order.

The waitress went away and came back with a basket of sliced focaccia loaf and a small dish of olive oil mixed with balsamic vinegar.

'Do you like to cook?' Stella asked, reaching for a slice of the crusty bread.

'The basics. Soup. Spag bol if I've got time. Skye cooks for the three of us sometimes — usually when my mum sends me back to Edinburgh with half her larder and I've no idea what to do with it. She'd be horrified if she knew how often I eat ready meals or takeaways.'

'Microwaved scrambled eggs on toast for me.' It was Stella's turn to be rueful. 'Alice taught us both to cook but it's too much effort to go to for one. By the time I get home I can't be bothered.'

There she went again, sounding sorry for herself. 'If I have friends round I make more of an effort.' Well, at the moment there was a congenial flatmate and they pooled their resources sometimes. And she'd had Jane and Nathan from the office over, and Nathan on his own.

'Do you like living in London? I've been a few times — holidays, and for work.'

'I love my job. It can be very stressful but it's a real high when it goes well. And then you start all over again.' She smiled at Isabel. 'It's incredibly crowded of course — like Edinburgh in the Festival, but all the time. But I think I've got used to that now.'

Isabel appeared to be considering her next words. 'Have you met anyone special in London — is there a man in your life?'

Stella looked out of the window, as if the answer to Isabel's question might be written in large letters on the wall. But all she could see were the potted trees in the little courtyard and couples, chatting and laughing, as they came nearer the door to read the menu board.

'Sorry. Don't answer that if you don't want to.' Isabel dipped her bread into the olive oil mix.

'There's a guy in my office. Nathan. We've been out a few times. It's not serious though.'

She felt bad saying that — he had been sweet when she spoke to him yesterday. 'I like him but . . . ' She raised her eyebrows.

'He doesn't set the heather on fire?'

Stella thought about Isabel's phrasing before she answered. 'Thank you,' she said to the waitress, as a bowl of pale orange gnocchi sprinkled with parmesan cheese and fried sage leaves was put in front of her. 'No, he doesn't.'

It was a strange expression when you came to think of it — in the real sense 'setting the heather on fire' wasn't a good thing; in the metaphorical sense it was. Someone who made the world light up — so yes, Ross had set the heather on fire for her. Until she put the fire out.

'He didn't understand when I said I hoped to be there for only a couple of years,' she burst out, as if Isabel had been privy to her thoughts. 'But how could he understand? I never explained the reason.'

Isabel lowered the forkful of risotto she was about to eat, and waited.

'I didn't want to move to London, but I desperately needed the extra money.'

There. She'd said it. The words that shame and pride prevented her from saying to Ross fifteen months ago. That she'd never said to anyone else. They hovered in the air over the table. It was a huge relief to have them out after all this time. Perhaps now they would give her peace and stop going round and round in her head.

'Isabel, please eat. Don't let your risotto get cold. Can I tell you about it? You're such a good listener.' Stella made herself take a forkful of gnocchi and some wine. 'I didn't get the artistic gene. I always loved maths and I did accountancy at university,' she went on. If she were going to tell the story it would be best to start at the beginning. 'I don't know where that came from — it passed Alice and Maddie right by. I tease Maddie about it — she still counts on her fingers.'

Isabel laughed. 'I've seen her do that.'

'Alice lived — lives — frugally; she's never spent money the way other people do. I mean, hardly any new clothes, no foreign holidays or expensive meals out. Make do and mend and all that. Recycling before anyone else did. But it never occurred to me to think about her income, or lack of it.'

She took another gulp of wine. 'She'd been teaching art at the local high school but she gave that up when our parents died and we went to live with her. She started a pre-school art class in the house and did some adult classes too at the community centre but that was her only income. Her husband was a solicitor and a lot older than her — he left her money I think but that was thirty years ago. That old house always needs something done to it. We had to be clothed and fed. Educated. And there were always the waifs and strays. They had to be fed too.' Stella looked over at Isabel. 'That's what Maddie and I used to call them. Alice's artist waifs and strays. Lilias — I'll tell you about her sometime — is the latest in a long line. Anyway, what I'm getting at is, she never talked about money. I never thought about her finances.'

She stopped, remembering the moment when she was forced to think about them.

'But that's how it is, isn't it? Or how it should be,' Isabel interposed gently. 'Grown-ups take care of you, not the other way round.'

'But when I was older . . . anyway I was looking for an envelope in her desk and saw some paperwork from one of those money-lending companies. She owed thousands of pounds to them. I had to ask her about it. She cried — I'd never seen her cry before. It was harrowing.'

Alice had been burying her head in the sand for a long time and even with a sympathetic, if horrified, listener was reluctant to discuss it. She'd seen an advertisement, she said eventually, and the man sounded ever so nice when she phoned, went through all the forms with her.

It was after that bad winter a few years ago when one of the chimneys was blown down, and the gutters at the front of the house collapsed under the weight of snow; both had to be replaced. It hadn't felt like too big a loan to start with but then the letters came and the figures at the bottom got larger and larger and she didn't know what to do. She was so ashamed — she'd never been in debt ever before and the thought of telling anyone about it, well, she just couldn't.

'I got in touch with these people,' Stella said, 'but what were they going to say? Alice had signed the papers. It was all legal. The very next day my firm offered me a promotion, if I went to the London office. I would have turned it down — I didn't want to move so far away from Alice and Maddie and . . . and Ross. But there it was, like a godsend. The upshot was that I said I would pay it off. Even though London's so expensive to live in, I worked out that with the much higher salary and if I spent the minimum, I should be able to pay off a fair bit every month. Alice didn't want me to, of course. Said she would sell Hill View and move to a flat. But I knew that would break her heart. Mine and Maddie's too.'

She put her finger to her lips for a moment. 'Please keep this to yourself. We never told Maddie about why I went to London. I knew she'd be so upset and she wouldn't be able to keep it to herself. I hated having to prevaricate over why I was going. And Maddie of course couldn't understand why moving to London meant breaking up with Ross. And he thought I was interested in my career to the exclusion of everything else.'

'And you couldn't tell him?'

'Of course I wanted to. But it wasn't about me. I didn't want him and, inevitably, Gray, to know that Alice was . . . that we were in this predicament.'

Even though, as she'd said to Gray yesterday in the car, she thought of him almost as a member of the family, she couldn't tell him. If Alice had wanted him to know she would have told him herself. This was something Stella could and would sort out.

Stupidly, she'd thought that somehow Ross would understand and put their future on hold for a couple of years. But, not being in possession of all the facts, he hadn't. He couldn't.

And even though she'd managed to pay off a chunk of the debt, that wasn't the end of it. Alice's financial prospects were unchanged.

185

Pete had indicated she was doing well and would get more responsibility. Stella had to face up to the fact that her foreseeable future was in London.

She ate some of the almost cold gnocchi. 'You must be wishing you hadn't come out with me, Isabel. Let's change the subject. Tell me more about your plans for the Christmas break.'

10

It was hard to choose small presents for Isabel and Skye — Isabel worked in this department store, and Stella had no idea what would appeal to Skye. She settled on a selection of artisan chocolate bars for each of them — surely you couldn't go wrong with chocolate.

She was on her way to the ground floor when a dark red quilted jacket almost jumped out at her from a rack in the outdoor wear department. When she tried it on it fitted perfectly, and it was so warm and such a cheerful colour. She felt guilty as she handed over her credit card; she shouldn't be spending money on herself unnecessarily. Well, it was too late to worry about it. She asked the assistant to cut the labels off so that she could wear it right away and got on the escalator quickly to avoid any further temptations.

'Stella! Stella!'

Someone was waving frantically at her from the up escalator.

Carol. Last seen with Gav outside Harmony House after their wedding reception, their guests, including Ross and herself, running after their car, blowing kisses and hurling confetti . . . Stella little knowing that before the night was over she and Ross would be history.

She remembered with a pang that Carol did try to keep in touch with her. When she and Gav came back from their honeymoon and found out about the split between their two friends, Carol had contacted her immediately. But, as she'd had to be with everyone else, Stella was evasive about what had happened. Continuing to see Gav and Carol wasn't really an option when Gav and Ross were best mates. So although Carol had tried several times after that to talk to her Stella could not be any more forthcoming and eventually Carol had stopped calling.

It was to her great credit, then, that she was greeting Stella in a friendly way.

Stella waved back and pointed, indicating that she would follow Carol back up.

'Stell! Couldn't believe it when Gav said he'd seen you. Didn't believe him but his sister said, yes, it was you. Ross's mum told her. Sorry to hear about your granny's accident. How is she? And is it true Maddie's in Australia?'

Yes, same old Carol, apparently unchanged by marriage and motherhood, and holding no grudges against her friend.

'Hold on.' Stella laughed. 'It's lovely to see you, Mrs Armstrong! How are you? Congratulations on your baby. What did you have?'

'I had Emily, Emily Anne. She is *gorgeous*. Wait till you see her. She's in the café with my mother — Mum's come down to us for Christmas. We're doing last-minute present shopping and getting some bits and pieces for the babe. You've no idea how much stuff you need for someone who's this size.' She held up her hands about twelve inches apart. 'You haven't answered any of my questions. Is your granny all right? She fell, didn't she?'

Stella brought her up to date on what had happened to Alice.

'Where were you going now?'

'On my way out of here,' Stella said. 'Another few seconds and we'd have missed each other.'

'Do you have time to come to the café and I'll introduce you to my daughter? And I'm not letting you off the hook — I want to know what's happening in Stellaland and if you and Ross are back together. Gav's sister says he's as tight-lipped as ever on the subject.'

'We're not together. We ran into each other by accident yesterday. I suppose it was good to get it over with — it would be impossible to keep clear of each other forever. But nothing has changed.' Stella reached out to touch her friend's arm. 'How amazing to hear you say 'my daughter'! Imagine you being a mum. I'd love to see her.'

'Great. Come on. We can have a catch-up.' She checked her watch. 'Well, a short catch-up. We have to head back because . . . ' She stopped. 'I have to get back,' she repeated. 'You know, ever since I heard you were here I've thought of calling you. What were you planning to do for Christmas? Spend it with Lilias?'

Stella shook her head. 'I don't — '

'Not in Edinburgh surely? Turkey slices for one? Pull a cracker with yourself? You can't do that! Or are you going to Ross's grandpa's? I s'pose that would be tricky. You'd be *very* welcome to come to us, we've got three bedrooms in our new place, loads of room if you want to stay.'

She was still talking when they arrived at the table where her mum sat, surrounded by parcels, and beside a baby buggy.

'Mum, this is Stella. Do you remember? She was at our wedding in an *amazing* green dress.'

'Hello, Stella.' Carol's mum held out her hand. 'Yes, of course. You go out with Gav's friend Ross, don't you?'

There was an embarrassed pause.

'Sorry. Have I put my foot in it?'

'Yes, Mum, you have. But you weren't to know.' Carol bent over the pram. 'Moving swiftly on . . . Stella, this is Emily. Emily, this is Stella.'

Stella peered in past a dangling Christmas reindeer. Above a pale yellow blanket there was a small head with a lick of fair hair. A mini Carol. Her rosy little lips were parted as if she would like to speak — yes, definitely like Carol — but her eyes were tight shut.

'Well, that's very rude of you, Emily Anne,' Carol said fondly. 'Not to wake up and say hello to your Auntie Stella.'

Stella would have liked to stroke Emily's round cheek but was afraid she would be startled. 'She's lovely, Carol. So sweet.'

'Isn't she?' said Emily's proud grandma. 'Stella, I remember now. Your granny was at the wedding too, wasn't she? We had a nice chat.'

Stella explained about Alice.

'I'm sorry. It's a difficult time for you. Do give her my best wishes,' Carol's mum said sympathetically. 'You wanted to get back for two, didn't you?' she said to her daughter. 'You've got — ' She broke off.

'Yes.' Carol bent over the baby to tuck the blanket in. 'Stella.' She spoke without turning round. 'If you're at a loose end why don't you come down to Melrose with us? We could have a late lunch and then Gav could run you to Tweedbank for the train — or he'd take you up to the Infirmary. He's not at the garage this afternoon — he's working on a car we have up at the house.'

'I'm not going to the hospital this afternoon — Alice is having a scan. But haven't you got other plans?'

'We're just going home. Do come.'

'Are you sure Gav wouldn't mind? Driving me, I mean?'

''Course not. I've got him well trained. Besides, he'll be pleased to see you too.'

Carol's mum seemed to be signalling to her daughter with her eyes. Carol didn't respond. 'Then you can give Emily a cuddle,' she said to Stella enticingly.

Perhaps Carol's mum was worried that Gav, Ross's best friend, might not be as pleased to see her, nor want to be as helpful as her daughter assumed.

'But Gav — it will be awkward, won't it?' Stella said hesitantly.

Carol straightened up. 'It's none of our business whatever happened between you and Ross. He was obviously gutted but I very much doubt he's said anything to Gav about it — you know what men are like. It would be

192

great if you got back together but if that's not on the cards I'd be sorry if it meant that we didn't see you.'

So did Gav and Carol know anything about Skye? No doubt Ross would be 'tight-lipped' about her too but if she was going to be down in Melrose a lot it wouldn't be a secret for very long.

'I'm sorry you and I haven't been in touch,' Stella said. 'That was my fault. Things were . . . confusing. You're right — oh, not that there'll be anything different between Ross and me, but that shouldn't mean that I can't see my friends. I'd love to come, Carol, thanks.'

Carol's mum took charge of the pram as they moved towards the lift.

'Ross's restaurant is doing brilliantly,' Carol said. 'We haven't been since Emily arrived but we'll have her christening lunch in it — on the eighth of January. Will you be able to come? Once when we were there — it wasn't long after the new chef started — Maddie was in with friends, a flatmate I think and her old crowd from school. We had a fabulous meal — do you think you'll have a chance to go before you go back to London?'

'I don't think so.' Stella turned to face her. 'Carol, please, do you mind if we don't talk about Ross?'

'I'm sorry.' Carol didn't sound very contrite though. 'It's still hard to realise that you two aren't together. We're going this way,' she said, indicating right at the back door. 'I'm parked in the multi-storey at the back of the St James Centre.'

'Tell me about you and Gav,' Stella said. 'I understand that Gav's with his dad now, at the garage.'

'Yeah, they're really busy. The usual repairs and things plus they do up classic cars now — it's been a good sideline for them.'

'You've moved from the flat you were in?'

'When we knew that Emily Anne was on the way. A new house up the back of the town. It's got a garden and there are lots of young families around. It's great.'

'And what's it like being a mum? You look as if it suits you,' Stella said, as they crossed through St Andrew Square. There was an ice rink here too, and various bars and food stalls with fake snow sprinkled on their roofs. From somewhere came a tinkling 'Jingle Bells'.

'Love it. Love it.' Carol stroked Emily's little hand which was gripping the silky edge of her knitted blanket. 'And Gav's besotted too. Yes, I thoroughly recommend it.'

'Here we are.' Carol's mum spoke loudly and brightly as though she thought her daughter was being a little tactless in promoting motherhood to someone in no position to think about it herself. 'Carol, do you mind? I want to pop in and get some wool in Lewis's. I hope I won't be long — I remember which floor you're parked on.'

Carol lifted Emily out of the buggy and put her in a seat in the front of the car. 'Mum's already knitted enough outfits and blankets for a dozen babies,' she laughed, as her mother dashed off. 'Excuse me a sec, Stella.' She took out her phone and composed a couple of texts, hesitating over the wording of the second one before hitting send. 'Now I want to hear about life in the big city,' she said, as she deftly folded up the buggy and put it in the boot. 'Do you like it? Where do you live? Perhaps we could come down for a holiday sometime — you could show us round. I'd love to do the whole tourist thing. Have you made lots of friends?'

Stella was still answering Carol's questions when her mother arrived back, and they drove down the car park ramp. She didn't think Carol would be interested in the minutiae of her job so she told her about the London sights she'd seen and about the area she lived in, a part of the city that not so long ago would have been cheap to rent in but was now mind-bogglingly expensive, like every-where else.

'And friends?' Carol persisted.

'I've got great colleagues and some of them have become friends.' Stella debated with herself whether to throw Nathan into the conversation, to say that some of the London tourist landmarks had been seen in his company, hint about his Christmas invitation ... She remembered how, in the car on Wednesday, Ross had said, 'We didn't just drop her off, of course. We went into the terminal building with her, as far as we could go.' 'We'. Ross and Skye. Yes, she would talk about Nathan. It would be bound to get back to Ross and let him see that she was moving on too. That they could draw a line in the sand. While knowing that she herself was still behind that line.

She'd hardly embarked on the subject, was telling Carol and her mum about a visit to the Tower of London, when Emily decided to wake up and make her presence felt, which meant no one else could be heard. As Carol's mum cooed over the baby and, from the back seat, tried to soothe her, Stella realised they were passing the entrance to the Infirmary and blew a silent kiss to Alice, fervently hoping that her scan would show no lasting damage.

Carol put some Christmas music on to play. With the baby's wails and the songs as background to her thoughts Stella sat back in her seat and looked out of the window as the car sped towards Melrose.

★ ★ ★

Ross let himself into Gray's house.

'Grandpa?' No reply. He walked through to the kitchen. Out of the window he could see the shed door was open and inside it Gray was cutting wood for the stove.

'I can do that, Grandpa,' Ross said. 'You should let me know when you're running out of logs.'

'I can still do a pretty good lumberjack impersonation.' Gray grinned as he handed over the axe. 'That wood-burning stove fairly burns the wood and no mistake. It's a life's work trying to keep up with it.'

'It was supposed to make your life easier, not harder,' Ross said, taking off his jacket. 'I'll chop and you stack, okay?'

'Bette said you're seeing Gav and Carol this afternoon,' Gray said, as he added to the neat pile of wood at the back of the shed.

'The baby — *Emily* — is being christened next month and they're having lunch after in the restaurant, so we're going to talk about the food, whether they want a buffet or a sit-down.'

'How does Gav like being a dad?'

'Don't know. I've hardly seen him and when I do he's too knackered to speak. Goodness knows why. Don't babies that age sleep all the time?'

Gray laughed. 'As far as I remember they sleep a lot but not necessarily when you want them too. Well, that should be a lovely occasion — and it'll spread word about the restaurant too. You're doing really well there, lad, and in the shop, everyone says so.'

Ross felt a lump in his throat. 'Thanks, Grandpa.'

'Could you tell Gav I'll be bringing my car round to him next week? Engine's developed a cough of some sort. Getting old like myself, no doubt. Time I had a new one. I'd be glad of his advice.'

'I'll tell him. Shall I make you a cup of tea before I go?'

'No, don't worry. I'm quite capable whatever your mother might think. Maybe you could pop in later if you have time? Her and your dad won't be back until late.'

'I'll see. I'm hoping I'll be able to drag Gav out for a swift pint if he hasn't nodded off. And if Carol lets him. You could join us — shall I let you know if it's on?'

'I'd like that.' Gray clapped his hand on Ross's shoulder.

'Grandpa?' Ross put his hand over Gray's for a moment. 'When Dad comes back and he and Mum leave, shall I move back in here? I'm thinking of doing up the flat and asking Tom if he'd like to rent it — he travels from Langholm at the moment.'

'I'm sure he'd go for that — that road's tricky this time of year and he'll be travelling it in the dark mostly.' Gray dusted his hands on his trousers. 'It makes sense for Tom but is it really what you want to do? Don't you want to be in your own place? Has your mother put you up to this? I've told her I don't need looking after.'

'No, she hasn't. Not at all. But she was talking about advertising for a housekeeper for you.'

'I heard her. A housekeeper! It's a ghastly idea. I don't want a stranger in the house and I'm perfectly — '

'I didn't think you'd like it,' Ross said, 'and if I said I was going to be here with you, Mum might get off your case.'

'Smart thinking.' Gray's eyes twinkled. 'Let's present a united front. It will be tough but we men shall prevail! But I'm still thinking it's not the best thing for you. Maybe we could divide the house in some way, have our own space as they say nowadays.'

'We'll talk about it.' Ross zipped up his

jacket. 'I'll let you know about that pint.'

Back out on the road he debated with himself whether or not to drive up to Gav's. The new housing estate was only half a mile's walk away — or run, but he wasn't dressed for running.

'Hey, Ross.' Two boys were coming towards him, one he recognised as living round the corner. 'This is my cousin. He's from Glasgow,' his young neighbour said. He nudged his cousin. 'Go on. Get his autograph. He got capped for Scotland.'

The other boy's eyes widened. 'Who did you play for? Was it Rangers?'

'Not football, you pillock.'

The cousin looked distinctly unimpressed.

Ross laughed. 'Sorry to disappoint you. We play rugby down here. But I like watching football.'

Ten minutes later, after a heated discussion on the merits of various teams, Ross headed towards the restaurant to pick up his car. He was running late; he'd have to drive now. Out of the corner of his eye he saw Carol's car turn up the road to the housing estate. An older lady sat behind her, probably her mum. He got a fleeting impression there was someone else in the back.

★　★　★

'Stella.' Gav kissed her on the cheek, rather coolly she thought. He wasn't surprised to see her — presumably one of the texts Carol had sent from the car park had been to him. Then he turned his attention to the car seat Carol was holding. He swooped down and unbuckled the straps.

'How's my best girl? Come to Daddy.'

Stella was amazed to see Gav suddenly so animated. He never used to be someone who showed his feelings easily but here he was, cuddling his baby daughter, his face all lit up, besotted, as Carol had said. Life certainly hadn't stood still since Stella left Melrose but why should she have expected it to?

Carol handed him a pink-spotted bag. 'Nappy time.' She turned towards Stella, laughing, as Gav bore Emily upstairs. 'Can you believe it? Gav, changing nappies. Now, come through to the kitchen, talk to me while I make a bite to eat. You were telling us about your friend Nathan and the Tower of London.'

Her mother was about to close the front door. 'Carol?'

Her voice sounded a little strained so Stella followed her line of vision.

Ross's car had drawn up.

'Carol?' Stella said in her turn. 'Did you know Ross was coming?' She found herself looking round the hall as if for somewhere to hide.

'We're going to have Emily's christening lunch in the restaurant. He's come to talk it through. I thought if you saw each other in company it might be easier for both of you.'

'I really wish you hadn't done that, Carol. Does he know I'm here?'

'Not yet.' Carol went to greet Ross at the door.

She meant it for the best. Stella knew that while at the same time being furious with her. And with herself. She'd walked right into that. To buy herself some time she went through the nearest door correctly assuming that it would lead into the lounge. Carol's mum followed her.

'I'm sorry,' she said. 'Carol can't resist trying to rearrange the world to her satisfaction. Especially if it's matchmaking between her friends. Look, Stella, of course I can leave you on your own here with Ross but I'm happy to stay if you'd like me to.'

'I would,' Stella said gratefully.

Ross could be heard talking animatedly in the hall while Carol, sounding more subdued than before, responded. She took Ross's jacket, told him Gav would be down in a minute and it sounded as if she was on the point of letting him know that Stella was here when he caught sight of her through the lounge door.

His face paled. He ran his hand through his hair — and then repeated the gesture. His way of buying time presumably. A lock of his hair remained standing on end.

Stella could only hope that he didn't think that she'd asked their friend to arrange this.

Carol put him right straightaway. 'Stella didn't know you'd be here, Ross. I'm sorry if I've done the wrong thing.' Her voice became louder, more upbeat. 'Guys, it's almost Christmas! Season of goodwill, remember? You're here now. Sit down and I'll make some sandwiches.'

Carol's mother leaped into the breach and made small talk. She told Stella about Emily's dramatic arrival two weeks before she was due, and Gav's midnight dash to get Carol to hospital; she asked her for more details about Alice and her accident; she discussed the weather forecast for Christmas; she said to Ross that she'd read a great review of the restaurant by a well-known local critic. Stella could have kissed her.

Ross could hardly not respond without appearing rude, but he managed not to look in Stella's direction during the entire conversation.

'Ross, mate, good to see you.' Gav was

downstairs again, carrying Emily. 'Come out the back and see this beauty Dad and I are working on. A Rover P4, 1962. Hang on, I'll get rid of this. Can you hold her for a minute?' He laid the baby on Ross's knee and went off to put the nappy bag in the bin.

Ross looked at Emily as if she might explode at any moment. Stella and Emily's grandma couldn't help laughing at his terrified expression.

'That's the way Gav was to start with,' Carol's mum said. 'He's an expert now. Put your hand behind her head. That's it. You're doing fine.'

Ross relaxed enough to catch a flailing little fist in his other hand. Stella's heart contracted. What a picture it made — the big man with the tiny baby in his arms; she found it hard to tear her eyes away. But if Ross were happy enough to be holding Emily, Emily herself would have none of it and roared her disapproval.

Her father came in and picked her up. She arched her back and howled even louder. Gav lifted her to his face and kissed her. 'Nothing I can do for you, my precious. You need your mum.' He bore her off to the kitchen. Ross nodded in the direction of Carol's mum and Stella and got up to follow him.

'Thank you,' Stella said. 'I'm glad you were here.'

'It's a shame,' Carol's mum said. 'I remember thinking you made a lovely couple at Carol's wedding. But things don't always work out, do they? And if you've met someone else in London . . . '

Through the door between the lounge and the kitchen Stella saw Ross miss a beat as it were; he seemed to pause for a moment between one footstep and the next. What had he made of that remark if he heard it? She wanted to say to Carol's mum, I made it sound different to the way it was. Yes, I was at the Tower of London with Nathan — but two others from the office were there too. They were all born in London but none of them had been before. It was a sort of jokey office outing.

'Excuse me,' Stella said. 'It was lovely to see you again.' She got to her feet and picked up her bag as Carol came through with the baby clamped to her chest.

'Peace reigns for the moment,' she said, sitting down carefully.

Looking through to the kitchen and out of the window Stella could see that the men were standing beside a car in a sort of makeshift garage. A roof stretched out from above the kitchen window, there were two rather flimsy walls and the fourth side lay open to the elements. Gav was talking, stroking the top of the car as if it were a cat.

'Carol, thanks for trying — I know you meant well — but this isn't going to work. Maybe I can see you on your own before I go back?'

'Definitely, but there's no need to leave now. I'll finish getting some food for us once this little madam's had some lunch.' The baby had one fist wrapped around Carol's finger, her eyes fixed on her mother.

'He doesn't even want to be in the same room as me,' said Stella. And that hurt so much. 'We have nothing to say to each other.'

'Oh you know what the boys are like when there's a car engine to strip,' Carol said. 'That's why he went out there with Gav.'

Secure in her marriage, Carol must have forgotten that life could be complicated and didn't always work out the way you wanted, and that a broken relationship couldn't be easily mended by a well-meaning friend trying to glue it back together over a plate of sandwiches.

'But Stell,' Carol went on, 'we won't be seeing Ross over Christmas. It'll be just family. Why don't you come to us? We'd love to have you, wouldn't we, Mum?'

'Yes, do,' her mother urged.

'That's really nice of you, but I want to be able to see Alice on Christmas Day.' She put up her hand to stop Carol saying what she knew was coming next. 'And no, Carol, you can't volunteer Gav or anyone else to take me up. I'll be fine, honestly.' She bent over to kiss her friend. 'Emily's wonderful. It's been great to see you. I'll call you later, shall I? Say goodbye to Gav for me.'

As Carol was occupied with feeding, so in no position to physically stop her, she could only continue to protest as Stella let herself out of the house.

She was thankful for the new jacket as she walked as quickly as her heels would allow back down the steep road into town — although a jacket with a hood would have been even better. Gloves would be a sensible idea too. A sleety wind blew straight into her face and whipped her hair around it. Her smart trousers were soon sodden and her legs very cold.

In the distance she could see the abbey, the ancient monastery where the heart of King Robert the Bruce was buried. It brought back a painful memory.

The day after Gav and Carol's wedding her heart had leapt when she saw she'd got a text from Ross. She'd spent the night trying to compose one to him and by midday still had not decided on what she would say. His was brief — *I can't believe last night happened, is there any point in meeting?* — but she sensed the anger behind it, imagined his finger stabbing out the letters.

She texted back to say she'd meet him at the café near the abbey. The walk there might clear her head. Give her time to decide what to say.

It was a vain hope. However much she went over it in her mind, the facts were the same. She had to go to London. She didn't want to tell Ross why. She pulled herself right back into a place where he couldn't reach her — a feeling she dimly remembered having when she and Maddie were told their parents wouldn't be coming back. After ten minutes he left her sitting there, both their coffees untouched, and the view of the abbey through the picture window became blurred by her tears.

It struck her now, as she came closer to it, that in all its ruined glory it could be a metaphor for her relationship with Ross.

★　★　★

There would be time, she suddenly thought, to go to Hill View, get dried off, changed into jeans and a jumper and boots. She couldn't remember exactly what was in her wardrobe there but it would be great to get out of her wet clothes. And to see Lilias of course. Thank goodness for Gray and Bette checking on her and keeping her up to speed on Alice's condition — it was impossible for Stella herself to communicate with someone who wouldn't answer the phone. But she couldn't help feeling rather guilty, as she thought of Lilias worrying about rats in the attic and rattling around in that big cold house by herself. Ross was right. The range had had its day and no longer heated the water adequately or kept the house warm enough.

Down in the square she looked at the bus timetable, working out her movements, then, as she turned away from it, she spotted Gray carrying a carton of milk on the other side of the road, his head down against the wind. An ancient waterproof hat was perched on top of his dandelion-clock hair.

'Gray!'

He couldn't hear her. She crossed over and came up behind him, caught his arm gently.

He turned round in surprise. 'Stella, how lovely! Where did you spring from?'

'I bumped into Carol in town. She asked if I'd like to come down for the afternoon — Alice is having a scan — I drove down with her — '

'And she took you to her house and Ross turned up.' Gray was quick to put two and two together. 'He told me he was going. And you ran away, eh?' He tipped up his head to see her better, making raindrops fly off his hat in all directions.

Stella didn't answer. She was colder than she ever remembered feeling in her whole life, and it wasn't only because of the weather.

'Lassie, you're shivering.' Gray put his arm round her. 'It's not a day to be hanging around at bus stops. Come back with me for a cup of tea.'

Stella leaned against him for a moment. 'I was checking the bus times. I thought I'd go to Hill View, find some of my winter woollies. I only have London clothes with me!'

'I'll come with you, shall I? Oh, isn't that Gav?'

A car drew up beside them and Gav lowered the window. 'Stella, Carol sent me after you. I was going to give you a lift to the hospital — I'd be happy to take you into Edinburgh now.'

'Gav, I'm sorry to be such a nuisance.' She thrust her hands deep into her pockets and tried to keep her teeth from chattering. 'Please go back. I'm going home now — to Hill View — to pick up a few things.'

Gav looked at Gray as if asking for guidance.

'Good of you, Gav,' Gray nodded. 'But Stella'll get back to Edinburgh later. I'll see she's okay. She's had a tough time.'

Gav's expression showed relief but also concern. 'Of course. Well, if you're sure,' he said, sounding warmer than when he'd greeted her earlier. 'I hope Mrs Greenlaw is on the mend, Stella. Give her our best.'

'I'll phone Carol later,' she said, as the window slid up again.

'Let's get you home,' Gray said. 'You need to get dry. And I'm sure Lilias will be glad of some company this stormy afternoon.'

* * *

'I know you meant it for the best, but it was never going to work,' Ross said. 'I've told you, Carol. It's finished between Stella and me.' He and Gav had been admiring the Rover's bodywork when Carol came out and told them that Stella had left. Clearly it was because of him being here. He realised that part of him had hoped that she'd asked Carol to set up a meeting, if only to give him the satisfaction of walking out on it himself.

When he saw her there, so unexpectedly, in that dark red jacket she hadn't had time to

211

take off, he was reminded of the dress in a similar shade that she wore that Christmas Eve, the night their eyes met under the mistletoe and their lips followed suit . . .

'Ross, I'm sorry, it was thoughtless of me.' Carol walked up and down with Emily, covered in a shawl, over her shoulder. 'Don't be mad. We haven't seen you for ages and we've got the christening to discuss.' She patted the baby's back. 'But I'm worried about Stella. Gav — could you go after her? Pretty please? See she's all right? I would go myself but Emily's only had half her feed.'

Gav raised his eyebrows at Ross who smiled ruefully back. Over the last fifteen months Gav had never mentioned Stella's name, not after Ross made it clear that the subject was off limits. So conversations with him were straightforward, not like the minefields Ross seemed to have strayed into during the last few days.

'Okay,' Gav sighed. 'This is another fine mess you've got us into, my sweet. Perhaps it will teach you to mind your own business. Although I doubt it. Right,' he said to Ross as he opened the bonnet of car, 'there's something you can do for me. I'll show you. And then I'll go and find Stella, although what I'm going to say to her I have no idea.'

'Thank you, darling.' Carol pouted a kiss at

him. She began to unbutton her blouse as she turned to go back inside.

Ross crouched under the bonnet with Gav. It was indeed a beauty of a car he was working on, its engine complicated in some ways but blessedly uncomplicated in others. You knew where you were with an engine. He'd always enjoyed going round to the Armstrong's garage with Gav after school and they were allowed to watch the mechanics working, even help, as long as they didn't muck about. Years later when he got his first car he was surprised at how much useful information he'd absorbed about how they worked.

Gav pointed out what he'd like Ross to do while he was away. When he'd gone Carol's mum came out with a cup of tea and a chocolate biscuit. He wanted to ask her what she'd meant when she said to Stella: 'And if you've met someone else in London . . . ' At least, the words were clear enough but he wanted to know more. That must have been a right old gossip the three women had on the way down here. Well, if he knew Carol it would all spill out at some point.

He bent over the engine and concentrated on the task in hand.

If he took life an hour at a time he'd get through it.

* ★ *

In a surprisingly short time, Gav was back. Merely saying, 'Stella's with your granddad,' he picked up an oily rag and leaned in alongside Ross, polishing the carburettor until it gleamed.

Carol came out, wearing a coat. 'It's freezing out here.' She put her arm round Gav's waist. 'Thanks, love. How was she?'

'Fine. With Gray.' Carol evidently decided, for once, that discretion was the better part of valour, and didn't ask any more questions. She perched on the car bumper, oblivious to Gav's protests. 'Mum's doing the lunch. Emily fell asleep before her feed finished so she could wake up any minute,' she said. 'Carry on, boys. You both look so industrious. Rossie, can I ask you about the christening now, before Miss Armstrong requires my presence again? You can multi-task like we women do.'

Ross stood up and rubbed his back. 'Fire away, Mrs Armstrong,' he said. You couldn't be cross with Carol for long. 'Is that a list of questions?'

'A list of *suggestions*.' She flourished a sheet of paper. 'Right, church finishes at twelve-thirty, allow half an hour for folk to coo over Emily, so we'll be at the restaurant

214

around one. Fortyish people. Okay?'

'Okay, so far.'

'I thought a buffet so folk can mingle more easily. A whole salmon, a ham, something veggie, two or three salads — one of them potato, it's Gav's favourite — a couple of puds, maybe a pavlova and a lemon tart? And Gav's sister is making a fabulous pink and white cake to have with coffee.'

Ross grinned at her. 'What have you left for me to do, Carol? You wouldn't like to come and run the restaurant for me, would you?'

'I like to be organised.' Carol swatted him with the paper. 'It's going to be a very special day. How much would that come to?'

Ross reached out. 'Can I take your menu plan? I'll send you some figures — and costs for fizz or wine?'

'Not so organised then, Car!' Gav teased. 'You forgot something to toast the baby's health.'

'It's because I'm not drinking at the moment,' Carol defended herself. She got off the bonnet. 'That's Mum waving at me. I better go. And you two come and have your sandwiches. How long can you stay, Rossie?' she asked, leading the way indoors.

'Not long, Carol. Difficult to have a social life with a restaurant. And Tom's away at a wedding today so I need to get back well before we open. Can I drag your husband away for a quick pint after we've eaten here?'

Carol waved her hand. 'Feel free. Who's cheffing today then?'

'Friend of Maddie's. Skye. She — '

'Did I meet her when she stayed with Maddie's gran? Pretty? Kind of bouncy?'

'If you say so.' Ross headed off any more questions — he could see Carol's mind going into overdrive as usual. 'Pint, later, okay Gav?'

'Actually, no, sorry. If you two would let me get a word in. I think I've got a buyer. Someone's coming round at four to check out the old girl.' He inclined his head in the direction of the car. 'After Christmas, though, mate. Definitely. Well overdue, that pint.'

'I'll text you next week then, fix a time.' Ross felt deflated. He'd been looking forward to talking cars in the pub with Gav — and Grandpa of course. He could still see if Gray felt like coming out but it hadn't been a definite arrangement, and anyone with any sense would be staying in on a day like this. And, hang on a minute, Gav had said Stella was with his grandfather. So he definitely wouldn't be going over there — it would appear as though he was chasing after her. He'd see Gray later though, after the restaurant closed, when he went home to

Priorsford Road, and his mother and father would be back from the west coast.

'Great to see you both — and to meet Emily,' he said, as he took his leave. 'She's a poppet.'

'Oh Rossie.' Carol put her arm through his. 'I'd hoped — '

'Yes, well.' Ross kissed her cheek. 'Thanks for the sandwiches.'

'I know I'm an interfering bat,' she said, holding on to him as he went out to his car. 'But I was thinking about you when I was feeding Emily. You and Stella. If you were quite indifferent to each other I'd believe it when you said it was all over. But it seems to me that your feelings, both of you, are as strong as they ever were — they're just not, not — '

'Just not good feelings?' Ross suggested sarcastically, getting into the car.

'Two sides of the same coin,' said Carol.

Ross caught sight of himself in the rear-view mirror. Why had no one told him his hair was standing on end? 'I'll be in touch about the christening.' He pulled the door to and managed a brief smile before driving off.

11

Lilias was pathetically glad to see them.

After the first flutter of greetings she started on a litany of anxieties. It would be earlier than usual but should she shut the hens inside? Otherwise, might they blow away in the wind? Or maybe their feathers would get so wet they wouldn't be able to hop onto their perches? With Maddie now being away would dear Alice and Stella be here for Christmas? She'd found an old paraffin heater — did Gray think she could use it to heat her bedroom? The man had delivered the Christmas tree and dear Ross had put it in its pot but how should it be decorated?

Stella left Gray explaining that paraffin heaters, especially old ones, should most certainly not be used, and made for her bedroom, now desperate to get out of her clammy trousers and shirt.

She paused for a moment in the front hall. As Lilias said, the tree had been delivered, and was in its pot, not left to lie on the floor as she had feared. But would there be any point in decorating it? Alice would be in hospital for Christmas — at least the staff hadn't indicated otherwise; she herself would therefore be in Edinburgh; Maddie would be eating barbequed prawns and acquiring a sun tan on a beach thousands of miles away; and Lilias would be going round to Priorsford Road on Christmas Day. She'd see Bette's lovely tree.

Upstairs, she towelled her hair and, thankfully discarding her wet clothes, changed into thick socks, jeans, a long-sleeved t-shirt, and a jumper — a Christmas jumper; a present from Maddie last year. There was no law to say they could only be worn on Christmas Day!

Her room was as she had left it fifteen months earlier, although either Alice or Lilias must have been in with the vacuum cleaner otherwise it would be like Miss Havisham's boudoir, covered in cobwebs and dust.

But why was she comparing herself with Charles Dickens's doomed bride? Feeling much more cheerful now that she was warm and dry she gathered some more clothes together to take back to the flat. There was a moment's disquiet when she came across the long green dress bought for Gav and Carol's wedding, and the dark red one she'd worn that Christmas Eve party. She moved them to the back of the wardrobe, out of sight.

On her way downstairs she paused outside Alice's bedroom door. It was strange, after all these years, to learn something of Alice's past; a small glimpse — and she hoped she would soon find out more — into the life of someone she thought she knew so well. How must it feel for Alice to have the past catch up with her? It would be lovely in a way of course with the prospect of Charlie being back in her life, but then also she would have the circumstances of their separation brought to her mind afresh.

She pushed the door open. How many times had she been in this room? Hundreds? Like the rest of the house it had heavy, old-fashioned furniture — Hill View had been in their grandfather's family for several generations — and was cluttered with pictures and ornaments. Maybe she could persuade Alice to have a massive tidy-up some time — she was probably so used to her surroundings that she didn't really see them any more. After being away for fifteen months and living with hardly any possessions Stella was struck by how much *stuff* there was in this house.

The other day, when she grabbed the nighties — had there been a black and white photograph in that drawer? There was something small and papery that had been dislodged from the back in her haste; she only glimpsed it as she banged the drawer shut. It wouldn't feel right looking through Alice's things — not that Alice would give two hoots — so if there wasn't a photograph in that drawer, or if there was but it had nothing to do with Alice as a child, she would look no further.

There was. And it did. It was definitely Alice. Two long pigtails. Big dark eyes. Sitting cross-legged on the floor, a small child, a baby really, on her lap. She was smiling for the camera — for the person who probably said 'say cheese' — but the boy was looking up at her, an adoring look on his little face. In one hand he clutched the end of a pigtail.

Was that all Alice had — all that was tangible — to remind her of her baby brother? Stella guessed so because the picture was so creased it must have been pored over, cried over, countless times. She made a mental note to get a copy made of it — no, two copies, a fresh one for Alice and one to send to Charlie.

She returned it, placing it at the back of the drawer with a small book of poetry on top to keep it flat.

Downstairs, there was no one in the kitchen, except for Patch asleep in his basket, but judging from the squawking noises outside, Lilias and Gray were giving the hens an early night. She filled the kettle and put it on the range and had a look round for something to eat — in her hurry to leave she'd missed the lunch Carol had been preparing. This was still her home but with Alice not there it felt weird to be looking in the fridge and in the big cupboard, averting her eyes from the large damp stain on one wall.

There was a loaf of homemade bread, nubbly brown. She cut a couple of slices and put them on top of the range too — they would take an age to be ready but she remembered how crisp and delicious toast was when it was made that way. Perhaps Lilias and Gray would like some too, she thought, as they came back each wrapped up in an old raincoat.

'I didn't have any lunch, I'm starving!' she said.

'My dear!' Lilias exclaimed. 'What can I get you?' She disappeared into the cupboard and emerged with three jars of jam. 'Strawberry, plum, blackcurrant?' She put them on the table and prepared to dive back for more. 'And there's — '

'Plum will be perfect, thank you, Lilias. You sit down. Shall I make some toast for you? Gray?'

It was almost like old times, when she and Maddie came home from school and they would sit round the kitchen table with Alice, eating toast, and telling her about their day. Different company this time, but Alice's jam, made with fruit from the tree in the garden, was as delicious as it had always been, and Lilias's bread was scrumptious.

Suddenly Stella knew what she should do now.

Of course she couldn't leave the Christmas tree undecorated; what was she thinking? It would be letting Alice down. And hopefully it would give pleasure to Lilias — she was in fact, in her own way, holding the fort here at Hill View; it would be a small thing to do for her in return.

'Right,' she said, turning round from the sink as she washed her sticky fingers. 'Christmas tree decorating party!'

'Oh yes.' Lilias clapped her hands. 'What fun!'

Alice's tree was always a very tall one, extending up the stairwell — the hallway's ceiling was also the top of house, with its cupola to let in light.

The tree would be barer than usual because neither Alice nor Maddie were here to add their extra embellishments, but that couldn't be helped. There were the eighteen glass balls with scenes of the nativity inside. Stella carefully hooked them over the

223

branches, guided by Gray and Lilias, who stood at a distance to take in the tree as a whole, so that they would be evenly spread.

No tinsel — Alice didn't like it — but there were strings of white fairy lights.

'Plug them in before you put them on the tree,' Gray advised. 'We'll need to check they're working.'

Disappointingly — she was excited, now she'd started, to see the tree all gorgeous and Christmassy — nothing happened when she switched them on so Gray bore them off to the kitchen table to patiently check each bulb.

'I'll get the ladder,' Stella said. She'd need to climb up on something to be able to drape the lights — if Gray got them to go — from the top and work her way down.

Lilias gave a wail. 'Not that ladder, please. The one that dear Alice . . . it was all my fault. Not the ladder. I'd be so worried you'd fall too.'

'Lilias.' Stella took her hand. 'It must have given you such a fright when it happened. But it certainly wasn't your fault.' She should have reassured Lilias about that the other day. 'You know Alice — even if you hadn't been with her she'd have tried to put the picture up. She does it all the time. She could have lain there for ages — thank goodness you were here.'

'That's true, that's true, I hadn't thought of it like that. That's such a comfort, Stella dear. I promise I'll hold on to the ladder very tightly this time and of course dear Gray will help.'

'Is it in the cupboard off the back corridor?' That was where it usually lived.

Lilias nodded.

'How did — ?' Stella stopped. Of course, Ross would have put it back for Lilias; she'd never have managed it on her own. 'I'll get it,' she said before Lilias could embark on more stories of dear Ross's helpfulness.

It wasn't a light, modern, metal ladder but an old wooden one, very heavy, a struggle to remove. It made a loud scraping noise along the floor as she reversed out, the cupboard door behind her blocking the corridor. She wasn't aware that the back door had opened until someone said, 'Lilias? Are you all right?'

Stella froze, half in and half out of the cupboard.

'Lilias?'

'It's not Lilias. It's me.' She pushed the ladder back in so that she could step out from behind the door.

'What are you doing here?' Ross's jaw slackened in surprise.

'I could ask you the same question.'

'Gav said you were with Grandpa.'

'I am. He's in the kitchen.'

'Why?'

'He's mending our fairy lights. Why are you here?'

'All that rain. I thought I'd check the attic — the buckets I put under the gaps in the roof.'

'Thanks.' She hoped her grudging tone conveyed her dismay over his reminder of the house's defects, their beholdenness to him, the fact that he was here at all. She turned so that her back was to the wall to allow him to walk past her down the corridor.

He didn't. 'What was that horrible noise?'

She sighed inwardly at the inevitability of what would happen next. 'I was trying to get the ladder out of the cupboard. For putting the lights on the tree. Alice has excelled herself this year. You've seen it — it must be nearly three metres high.'

If there was the tiniest glimmer of laughter in his eyes it was gone in a flash. 'Shall I help you?' he asked, not making any move to do so.

'If you have time. I'm sure you have better things to do.' She gestured for him to pass her so that she could open the cupboard door again. Why on earth it had been designed to open out rather than in, she couldn't imagine. It was extremely inconvenient.

It took some manoeuvring by Ross to get the ladder through the house to the front hall. Stella shuddered at the thought of her granny and frail Lilias doing the same thing — no wonder they were both shaky by the time they came to actually use it.

Lilias, of course, exclaimed over Ross's presence, her worries over Stella's safety put to rest now that there would be two men here to steady the ladder.

Gray appeared from the kitchen, with an armful of starry-shaped bulbs and wires. 'Ross! I thought I heard you. These are fixed now, Stella. Let there be light!'

Ross took off his jacket and hung it over the banister. 'Do you want me to put the lights on or hold the ladder?'

Neither, she wanted to say. I want you to go away.

'Hold it, please. Oh, just a minute.' Stella went to retrieve the old shoebox, home to the Christmas fairy. She handed it to Lilias. 'Perhaps you could unwrap the fairy, pass her to me when the lights are on?'

Gray looked up at her as she leaned this way and that around the tree and wound the lights over its branches, but after she'd accidentally met Ross's eye once he kept his gaze on the floor.

'Now.' She climbed the ladder again when

the lights were in place. 'Now, the crowning glory!' She reached down happily to take the fairy from Lilias but the older woman wasn't tall enough. Before Stella could come down a few steps Ross had taken the fairy from Lilias and was holding it up. He must have caught the end of her smile and probably it was an automatic response, but he smiled back. The fairy almost went to her doom on the flagstone floor as Stella fumbled over taking it from him. The movement seemed to become suspended in time — her hand, his hand, the Christmas fairy held by them both.

She wanted the moment to be over and she wanted it to last forever. The smile had confirmed to her what she knew already, that there could never be anyone but Ross for her. But he let go of the fairy and turned away, and there were Gray and Lilias looking up at her, waiting expectantly for her to put it atop the tree.

The fairy's wings had become a little crushed over time and her stiff white skirts were no longer so white. But her expression was as sweet as ever and her wand still held the promise of a wish asking to be granted.

Alice was out of danger. Maddie was happy. Work — well, work was work. Nothing to do with magic. So there was only one desire to be fulfilled. *I wish that Ross . . .*

She blinked. Lilias had darted over to the wall and switched on the lights. Stella was planning to make more of a ceremony of it but never mind. The tree was for Lilias's benefit after all. *Did you get that wish? I never finished it.*

'Stella, lass.' Gray held her elbow as she reached the last step. 'It's five o'clock — I should have kept an eye on the time.'

Stella clapped a hand to her mouth. 'Oh no! I lost track myself. I'll never get to the Infirmary by six-thirty.' There were the clothes she'd looked out to retrieve from her bedroom, ten minutes to get to the bus stop — she tried to remember the bus times.

Gray and Ross looked at each other in wordless communication.

No, not another fraught car journey with Ross. That would be more than she could bear. 'I don't want a lift from you,' she said to Ross. 'I'll just have to be late.'

He looked at her briefly. 'I wasn't going to offer. I'm front-of-house in the restaurant tonight. And that's where I should be now. Lilias, I'll check the attic, shall I?'

Lilias followed him upstairs, talking about buckets and cloths.

'Right, my dear,' Gray said. 'I'll take you up.'

'You certainly will not,' Stella said. 'I

wouldn't dream of it.'

'It doesn't mean going through town, remember. I'd like to.'

'I can't let you — it's so horrible outside and, anyway, isn't it tonight that Kenneth's coming?'

'Yes, but I'll be home long before then. They won't be back until late, Bette said.'

'I'm still not happy about it, it's too much — '

'Perhaps they'll let me see Alice,' Gray interrupted. 'I know you said tomorrow but maybe they'll relent.'

She put her arms round him and gave him a hug. 'If you're sure then. It would be a real treat for her if you were allowed in to see her too.'

He held on to her for a moment. 'That wasn't so bad, was it?'

'What?'

'Being in the same room as Ross. No hard feelings, eh? So I'll come up to see Alice tomorrow afternoon as arranged and bring you back with me for Christmas with us?'

She disentangled herself. 'I don't think so, Gray. Not because of Ross.' Not *just* because of Ross. It would be impossible to spend a day that was supposed to be happy and jolly in his company. And the night before when Bette would have her party — that would be the worst way of spending Christmas Eve that she could think of. 'They're more relaxed about visiting on Christmas Day I think. I'll spend as much of the day as I can with Alice.'

'I could come and get you on Christmas afternoon then,' Gray persisted. 'I don't like to think of you going back to an empty flat.'

'Shall we see how Alice is, before making any plans?' she asked. 'But it's lovely of you to offer, I do appreciate it.'

Gray made a tutting noise as she went upstairs to fetch her belongings.

Lilias stood at the foot of the ramsay ladder that led up to the attic space.

'I'm going now, Lilias. Gray's taking me up to the Infirmary — he'll let you know tomorrow how Alice is.'

'Dear Alice, do give her my love. And tell her I hope she'll be home very soon. Ross,' Lilias called up, 'Stella's going now.'

Stella looked at her with exasperated affection. So much for hoping to leave without seeing Ross again. But he should probably be told that Gray had offered her a lift. She could hear him moving around.

'Fine,' he called back.

Evidently Lilias thought he hadn't heard her properly. 'Stella's leaving, Ross dear.'

Now his face did appear in the hatch. 'She's good at that.'

231

'What did you say, dear?'

'Nothing. I hope Alice is better.'

Before he disappeared again, Stella said, 'Gray is very kindly driving me up.' She turned to Lilias. 'I'll see you soon. And I'll tell Alice how well you're looking after everything.'

As she passed through the front hall she glanced up at the top of the tree. The sweet face stared straight ahead. Perhaps she was deep in thought about how to grant Stella's wish. Or perhaps she had decided that it was beyond the capabilities of even the most magic of Christmas fairies.

★ ★ ★

Stella pushed open the door of Alice's room to see an unknown lady in her bed. She retreated to the nurses' station in alarm.

'She's well enough to be in a ward now,' the nurse said, indicating which one.

Alice was sitting up properly. The bruise on her forehead had faded a little and was now purply rather than that frightening blue-black. Someone had brushed her hair and her brown eyes had something of their old sparkle. She was wearing the white nightie Stella had bought her; the new dark blue slippers with pink rosettes sat at the end of the bed.

Stella's spirits lifted at the sight of her. 'You look so much better. I've brought you some face cream and a lipstick — I hope it's the right shade.'

'Thank you, pet, how lovely. And for my nightie, it's ever so much more comfy than the hospital one, all open at the back.' She prodded the cage over her hurt ankle. 'Not sure when I'll be wearing the slippers — or slipper I should say. They might get me hopping tomorrow. You look very Christmassy! I remember that jumper. Now.' She reached for Stella's hand. 'I've had an idea.'

She *was* feeling better. Stella had been hearing Alice's ideas and seeing that gleam in her eye for as long as she could remember.

'Can I tell you something first?' Stella said. 'I ended up being in Melrose today, with Carol, and then Gray drove me up here. That's why I was late — we had to go really slowly because it's wet and misty. So Gray is downstairs and he'd love to see you. I had a word with the nurse and she said he could — but not the two of us at the same time. So I'll stay until about quarter to and I'll send him up.'

'That will be wonderful — make me feel I'm getting back to normal. Did you . . . did you see Ross?'

'In passing. Now, what's your idea?' She braced herself.

'I don't know what time it will be in Australia but do you think we could ring Maddie? If you have a number for her? And then maybe I could speak to Charlie!'

Stella looked around. The other three ladies in the ward were all in conversation with their own visitors and would not be disturbed by a phone call nor, she hoped, interested in eavesdropping on one.

But she still wasn't sure it was a good idea. 'Are you sure you're up to it?' she asked gently. 'I mean, I don't know yet what happened to separate you and Charlie but it must have been something traumatic. Do you want to think about it all before you're really better?'

'It'll make me feel better to speak to him.' Alice's eyes glistened with tears. 'I'll tell you about it, pet, but it's a long story and, yes, it's a sad one. I'm going to write what I remember down for Charlie, and for Maddie and you. It's all come back to me since I got his letter, as if it had happened last week.

'It wasn't uncommon you know, if parents couldn't cope for some reason, to give one of their children up for adoption. And my mother couldn't cope, not after my da came back from the war little more than a vegetable. It sounds as if it worked out well for Charlie. I so wish our mam could have known that.' She reached over to the locker for her glass of water and took a sip. 'But I'll skip to the happy ending! You know there are all these places now, on the Internet, where you can trace your ancestors and get certificates and things?'

Stella nodded. This was like the television programme Isabel had told her about.

'Well, I had a letter — was it two or three weeks ago? I can't remember — asking if I had been born Alice Dodds, daughter of Jack and Patsy Dodds, and if so, he was my brother, Charlie.'

Stella felt tears spring to her own eyes. 'That's just . . . after all these years.'

'He said he'd been adopted by lovely parents — he has their surname, Hollis — and any vague memories he'd had of his first two years faded. Even when he had children and then grandchildren himself he never wanted to find out where he'd come from. But a year ago he had a bit of a health scare — he didn't say what — and suddenly he thought he'd like to know more. All he can remember is our gran's cat and trying to say my name — he can't picture our mam at all. Isn't that sad?'

'And you wrote back?'

Alice looked down at the sheet and plucked at it with suddenly shaky fingers. 'I did but . . . I know it was rash but a letter seemed inadequate, so I sent an emissary as well! Having Charlie meet my granddaughter means a connection has been made between us at long long last.'

It did make a kind of sense. Stella couldn't begin to imagine how she would feel in the same position, or what she'd have done.

The question of how the fare to Australia had been paid for could wait; it certainly wasn't the moment to ask Alice, not when she was all set to speak to Charlie.

But Alice was still pleating the sheet. 'I put off telling you. Thought you'd be cross.'

'Cross? About what?'

'The money for Maddie's fare,' Alice said piteously. 'You don't fly. And of course you're so busy. And Maddie said she'd love to go. I borrowed it — not from those people though, don't worry.'

So Alice had asked Gray to lend her money — who else could she have turned to? At least there would be no frightening letters from him accumulating in Alice's desk. But did that mean that Gray now knew all about the sorry state of Alice's finances?

'Of course I'm not cross with you,' she said

softly. 'But I wish you'd asked me. I'd have paid for the fare.'

'No. When I think what you're doing for me. No. I couldn't ask you for anything else.'

But it would be Stella who would be paying the loan back. She'd have to know who it came from. Well, she'd shelve that problem until after Christmas — add it to the list.

'Shall we make that call?' She put her phone on speaker.

'Maddie? Mads? Did we wake you up? It's me, Stella. I'm in the . . . I'm with Alice.'

'Granny! How's your leg? I couldn't believe it when I heard you'd fallen. Charlie was really upset.'

Alice gave a little gasp of joy. 'Don't worry about me, pet. Tell me everything.' Although she could hear Maddie perfectly well Alice put her face close to the phone as if that would bring them physically nearer to each other.

'I will, I'm desperate to catch up with you both,' Maddie said, 'but I'm going to get Charlie. Luckily, he's an early riser.' There was laughter in the background then she said, 'Charlie's here, Alice, he's right here to speak to you.'

'Ally? Is that really you? This is your little brother.'

For a moment Stella thought that Alice

wasn't going to be able to reply but then she swallowed hard, cleared her throat, and put a bright smile into her voice. 'It is, Charlie, it's Ally. It's your big sister.'

Stella took the phone off speaker and put it into Alice's hand. This was a private moment for the two of them — as private as was possible anyway. She went to stand at the bottom of the bed, watching Alice's animated face. It would be so wonderful if she and Charlie could meet soon and catch up, as best they could, on the years since they last saw each other.

Gray came out of the lift.

'That call to her brother's done her a power of good, I think. It was all she could talk about. Monday, they're saying, all being well, for her getting out.' He sat down beside Stella. 'I'll run you back to Maddie's flat.'

'No. You must get home. I absolutely put my foot down this time, Gray. I'll get the bus. I refuse to get in your car. You can't make me!'

Gray laughed, holding up his hands. 'I give in.'

She put her head on his shoulder. 'What would the Greenlaw family do without you, Gray?' she asked softly. 'On top of everything else, to lend Alice the money for Maddie's fare. That was so good of you.'

Gray jerked upright. 'Maddie's fare? I didn't lend Alice any money, now or ever. What do you mean?'

'What? You didn't . . . then who did?'

'I have no idea. But why did she have to borrow? I — well, I'd never really thought about it. She lives so simply, never spends a penny on herself.'

'No, she doesn't but — '

'I think she got a decent price for John's business after he died,' Gray interrupted, clearly thinking aloud. 'And he'd inherited the house so there was no mortgage. I thought he left her quite well off. Although all that's years ago of course.'

'Maybe he did, but there's hardly anything left now. If it wasn't you, then who?' Stella burst into tears.

'Whoa, Stella, what's wrong? Is there something else — is this about more than Maddie's fare?'

And so Stella found herself, between gulps, and not leaving anything out, telling Gray the whole sorry story.

'Can I tell Ross?' he asked, eventually.

'No!' Stella implored Ross's grandfather. 'I didn't want him to know at the time. Alice was so upset and mortified, she didn't want anyone to find out, but I tried to somehow tell him without actually telling him — as if that was going to work — and we had a shouting match and neither of us backed down, and I'll have to own up to Alice now that I've told you.'

'Is everything all right?' a passer-by, maybe a nurse going off duty, asked in concern.

Stella nodded, as she tried to find a tissue in her pocket. 'Yes, thanks. Sorry,' she said to Gray. 'I'm making a spectacle of us both.'

'You're not, my dear, you're not at all.'

'It was unforgivable of me. I see that now. I couldn't bring myself to look at it from his point of view before. If anyone tells him it must be me. But it's way too late. He looks at me as if he hates me.'

Gray put his arm round her. 'You were thinking of Alice, trying to protect her, save her face. She's a hard person to help, isn't she? Always thinking of others first even though she's had such a lot of trouble in her life. But it's never too late. Never too late, Stella.' He pulled her closer. 'I came out of that lift never guessing I was about to find the answer to something that's bothered me these last fifteen months. You know, I should have realised there might be difficulties — Ross was saying that the house is looking pretty shabby these days.'

'We'll cope, don't worry.' Stella blew her nose.

' 'We' includes me now, Stella, don't forget. You don't have to keep all your worries to yourself any more. I wish there was somewhere we could have a cup of tea but the café's closed.'

Stella stood up. 'You must go — you have a long drive ahead of you.'

'I'll walk you to the bus stop.'

'Go! I'll walk *you* to the car. And I'll see you tomorrow.'

On the bus, huddled in a window seat to hide her tear-stained face, Stella remembered that she'd promised to phone Carol. She hoped now wasn't a bad time but when there was a new baby in the house maybe there wasn't a good time.

'Stella, I'm sorry, I was out of order today. Gav was furious with me. I Went Too Far, he said. In capital letters.'

'That's never happened before, has it! But Ross and I — it's not fixable, Carol. It's over.'

There was a burst of laughter from a crowd of people at the back of the bus.

'Where on earth are you?' Carol asked.

'On my way back from seeing Alice. She's on the mend, thank goodness. It's a long story about why Maddie's in Australia — a really amazing story. I'll tell you about it sometime. It means a lot to Alice.'

241

'How intriguing. And when will Maddie be back?'

'I don't know — we've spoken but that didn't crop up! Look, you're probably busy with Emily — '

'And Christmas?' Carol wasn't giving up easily.

'Just another day. No, I'll see Alice, phone Maddie, it'll be fine.'

'You know where we are if you change your mind. Oh, I said to Gav, couldn't he lend you a car? Then you could get down here easily.'

'Oh Gav — leave the poor man alone! He must be completely fed up with me. Anyway, the parking around Maddie's street is dire. It wouldn't be practical. But thanks for the thought, Carol. I'll be in touch. And yes, if I change my mind . . .'

She hoped it wasn't as misty as this on the way to Melrose. It wasn't a very long drive — it should take Gray about an hour and a half — but the road was twisty in places. She'd ring him later to say thanks again for driving her up.

What the repercussions would be of her meltdown, she didn't like to think. She would have to confess to Alice that her secret had been given away. How would Alice feel about that? Gray would keep it to himself but his concern for Alice, now that he knew, would show itself in a hundred different ways.

It would be great, cheer her up, to speak to Maddie again, she thought when she was back in the flat — they'd barely managed two words earlier. But when Maddie answered it didn't sound as if she was still in the house. There was the sound of a door clanging shut.

'Stell, are you still there? Sorry, I was in Briony's shop — she's one of Charlie's granddaughters. I've stepped outside.'

'A shop?'

'You'll never believe it — selling her own jewellery! And beautiful glass that her brother makes, and Charlie's watercolours, it's brilliant.'

'So they all got the artistic gene?' Stella felt fleeting regret that it had passed her by.

'Not all — a couple of them are quite normal! Stella, how is Alice, really? It all sounds a bit odd — is her ankle really bad?'

There was no point in mentioning the concussion, not now the worst had passed and the brain scan had showed nothing to worry about. 'It was a bad break. It will take a long time to heal — at her age.'

'I never think of her as being old. Anyway seventy-something is the new fifty, isn't it? Stell, what do you think of this?' It sounded as if Maddie was pacing up and down in excitement. 'After he spoke to Alice, Charlie told me that he's going to book for him and Jill, that's his wife, to fly to Scotland to see her, and if I change my flight time and stay out for another few weeks we'll all come back together!'

'Oh Mads. Alice will be, well, that'll mean the world to her.' Stella's mind raced ahead. She'd be back at work of course but she'd go up to Melrose for the weekend, and maybe their newfound relatives would like a few days in London as well. What an amazing reunion it was going to be. She imagined Maddie and Alice, perhaps Gray too, waiting at the airport. Would Alice be on crutches, in a wheelchair — ?

As her thoughts ran on Maddie interrupted them. 'Two other things. I'll take a photo of Charlie on my phone and send it to you. And Stell, I'm going to move back home, I've decided, and work from there. Charlie thinks I should open a shop, like Briony's, in Melrose. What do you think of that?'

★　★　★

One party was still in the dining room and they were at the coffee stage of the meal now. Ross sent the last waitress home — he'd clear the table himself.

The evening had been non-stop, a blur of

people and food and wine, and the noise of conversation and laughter. But all he could think about while talking and listening to his customers was Stella on top of that ladder.

He knew her smile was for Lilias, not for him, but he couldn't help returning it and basking in its warmth for a fleeting moment. She appeared to be much more happy and relaxed than she'd been earlier in the day before she removed herself from Carol's attempt to get them in the same room. And she was so lovely in that silvery green jumper with the stars on it — stars for Stella-star-of-the-sea. His Star. His ex-Star.

Years ago, when they were little kids, Stella and Maddie would ask their friends round for a tree-decorating party. All the girls would close their eyes tightly when Alice told them to ask the fairy to make their wish come true. The boys were more interested in the mince pies and homemade biscuits but there was one occasion when he'd made a wish, squeezing his eyes shut and opening them again quickly so that the other boys wouldn't notice. This afternoon, as she perched on the ladder, looking rather like a Christmas fairy herself, he wondered if Stella was remembering those parties and the faith that she and her friends evidently put in the power of a fairy's wand.

'I hope you enjoyed your meal.' He was on automatic pilot as the last guests asked for their bill.

'Delicious. We'll definitely come again. And I'd like to book to have my birthday dinner here.'

It was a reply he'd been hearing variations of all evening.

In the kitchen Skye was wiping down surfaces, and the teenager Ross employed as kitchen assistant was busy washing pots at the sink.

'That was very successful,' Ross told Skye. 'Pottery's gain is cooking's loss.'

'Phew! Thanks. It all passed so quickly. I was worried about the pheasant but all the plates were cleared so it must have been all right. Well, I'll be glad to get to my bed — I'm exhausted!' She paused. 'Unless you want to come up for a coffee?'

Ross put the last plates in the dishwasher. 'I won't if you don't mind,' he said. 'My dad's coming home tonight. I haven't seen him for three months.'

Skye pouted. 'Just a — '

A phone rang.

'I think that's yours,' Skye said. She pointed to his jacket hanging over the back of a chair. Ross felt in the pocket for his mobile and looked at the caller ID.

'Grandpa?'

'Ross.' Gray sounded strained. 'I had an argument with a fence post near Carfraemill.'

'You what? You've had an accident?'

'It was misty and the car was acting up. I was crawling along but I misjudged — look, I've phoned the police. I phoned home too but there was no reply. The police will probably give me a lift so — '

'I'm on my way.' Ross tried to put his jacket on and hold the phone at the same time. 'Where exactly are you, do you know?

'I've got to go,' he said to Skye when he hung up. 'My grandpa's crashed his car.'

Skye gasped. 'Where is he? Shall I come with you?'

'No, you — ' He stopped to reconsider. It might be useful to have someone else there plus it would be good to have company. 'Yes, thanks. I'd appreciate it.' He nodded to the pot washer. 'I've got to lock up now — leave everything.' He bundled them both out of the door.

'What happened?' Skye asked, as they sped out of town. 'Is it serious?'

'Don't know,' Ross said briefly. The mist had lifted and the rain had slowed to a fine drizzle. If he could go back to that moment when Stella had called up to the attic space to say that Gray was giving her a lift he'd

— well, what would he have done? He couldn't have stuck his head out and told her to get the bus, not in front of Lilias. He couldn't have driven her himself even if he'd wanted to. He could hardly tell his grandfather what to do or not to do. But hindsight is a wonderful thing — he should have done something to prevent this happening.

He put his foot down harder on the accelerator, as he thought of Grandpa, maybe injured, alone in the dark on a country road.

The police car had arrived just ahead of him by the look of things. One policeman, carrying a torch, was holding Gray under the elbow. Ross drove a little further on until he came to the bottom of a farm road where he could park safely, and ran back, not bothering to take the keys out of the ignition.

'Grandpa, are you all right?'

'Is this your grandson, sir?' the policeman asked. He looked more closely at Ross. 'It's Ross Drummond, isn't it? That was a great try you — ' He broke off, realising that this wasn't the time for discussing rugby tactics.

'Yes, of course it is.' Gray swayed on his feet and the policeman steadied him.

'I was about to take your grandfather's name,' the policeman said. 'Is it Drummond too?'

'Ramsay.' Ross took Gray's other arm.

248

'Graham Ramsay. 10 Priorsford Road, Melrose. He's my mother's father.'

'Airbag's not been deployed.' A second policeman scrambled out of the ditch with the news. Ross knew that meant that his grandfather had been travelling at less than thirty miles an hour. 'Car's in a bad way though, I'm afraid.'

'I'll arrange for it to be towed. Armstrong Motors — Gav Armstrong's a mate,' Ross said. 'Grandpa, I'll take you — '

'Just a minute. We need to ask Mr Ramsay some questions. I'll ask you to come and sit in the patrol car, sir.'

Skye hung on to Ross's arm as Gray climbed into the back of the police car. 'I suppose they'll have to breathalyse him.'

Ross had forgotten she was there. 'What a thing to happen. Do you want to go back to the car? Or have my jacket? It would freeze a brass monkey out here.'

'I should have grabbed my own jacket,' Skye said, shivering. 'You need yours — I will go back to the car if you don't mind. He looked really pale, didn't he, your grandpa?'

'Maybe it was the light from the torch,' Ross said, because he wanted to believe that himself. Thank goodness Grandpa had his phone — the farmhouse was at least a mile up that road if Ross remembered rightly, and he could have waited a long time for another car to come along.

He got out his own phone and arranged with Gav to have the car taken away in the morning — it wouldn't cause any harm leaving it where it was overnight, so he was assured.

'They're not giving me a cold cell for the night.' Gray managed a brave smile as he walked rather unsteadily over to Ross.

'That's fine, sir,' the policeman said. 'I'd get your grandfather home as soon as you can, Mr Drummond. He's had a shock.'

Skye was curled up in the front seat. She must have put the engine and then the heater on, for her own benefit, but Ross was thankful that it was warm in the car for Gray.

With his grandfather, seatbelt strapped, behind him, Ross turned the car for home, giving a wave to the policemen as he passed them. He turned his head briefly to the left. 'All right, Grandpa?'

'Ross.' Gray leaned forward. 'Can I ask you something?'

'I think it would be better if you sat back, Grandpa. Tried to relax. As the policeman said, you've had a shock.'

'No, I need to know something.'

'What is it?'

'Did you lend Maddie the fare to go to Australia?'

'What?' This was completely unexpected. Ross wondered if Gray had banged his head — if he was delirious. He found himself exchanging a look with Skye, her face reflecting his surprise.

'Did you, Ross?' Gray raised his voice, very unlike him.

'Did I lend Maddie the fare?' Ross repeated. 'No, of course not. I mean, I would have if she'd asked but . . . ' He tailed off, not having a clue where this was leading. 'Why?' He slowed down and looked at Gray in the rear-view mirror.

'It was something Stella said. She thought Alice had borrowed from me.'

'It was Alice who wanted her to go,' Ross said. 'Didn't she pay for it?' He knew better than anyone that although Maddie's earnings were on the rise she lived pretty much hand-to-mouth.

Gray shook his head vehemently. 'No, she didn't.'

'But what's the problem?' Ross couldn't make sense of it. 'Why are you worried about it, Grandpa?'

'Stella's had a hard time lately.' It sounded as if Gray was changing the subject.

'I know that. Alice's accident — '

'It's not that,' Gray interrupted. 'Not just Alice's fall. Ach, I've been an old fool, Ross. There's something I should have done a long time ago.'

'I'm not with you, Grandpa.' Gray had leaned back in the seat now and had his eyes shut. And if Ross didn't keep his eyes on the road in front of him there would be a second crash this evening. 'I think I should get you checked out by a doctor.'

'I don't need a doctor. Just take me home, lad. A night's sleep is all I need.'

Ross speeded up again, feeling out of his depth and hoping his parents would be home soon — he knew they weren't yet because they had to travel on that same stretch of road. He hoped they wouldn't see the back end of Gray's car — what a fright that would give them. But there wasn't any point in phoning them now — they'd find out soon enough and there was nothing they could do in the meantime.

Skye nudged him, looking at him with questioning eyes. He shrugged in return. Alice — or Maddie — had to borrow money to pay the fare. It was a small mystery, but for the life of him he couldn't see why Stella should have brought the subject up or why it had upset Gray so much.

★ ★ ★

It was after eleven when Ross heard Bette's car stop outside the house and he went to the front door to greet them. It wasn't the homecoming Kenneth, his father, should have had.

His mother rushed upstairs to check on Gray. Although Ross had told her that he'd looked in on him five minutes earlier and he was asleep, of course she wanted to see for herself.

'He seems all right, his colour and his breathing,' she reported. 'But whether he wants it or not I'll get an emergency appointment for him at the surgery tomorrow.'

Christmas Eve. Not the best way to have to spend it.

'I'll think I'll leave a message now,' Bette said. 'Get to the top of the queue.' She went to the phone in the hall. 'Didn't you see the light flashing?' she asked Ross when she returned. 'There's a voicemail from Stella asking Gray to call her when he gets back.'

'It never occurred to me to check,' Ross said. 'I knew you'd phone my mobile if you had to.'

After he'd seen Gray into bed — it was unnerving being in that role for his

253

grandfather — he'd made coffee for himself and Skye. He should have dropped her off first but his one thought had been to get Gray home, and then he didn't want to leave the house in case Gray needed him. Of course Skye could have walked to the flat herself but she showed no sign of wanting to leave and he could hardly turn her out into the dark in a place she didn't know. So they sat on the sofa, she with her legs tucked up underneath her. He didn't want to talk about the crash or about anything else so he flicked through the TV channels until he came across a rerun of *Friends*. From Skye's reaction he gathered that she was a fan so he left it on but although he pretended to watch it his thoughts were a long way away from Manhattan.

Now he looked at his mother pleadingly. 'Can you phone her back?'

'She'll be upset,' Bette said. 'All right, I will, if you're sure you don't want to?'

'I'm sure.' He felt obscurely guilty. Earlier, in his head, he'd been practically blaming Stella for Gray's accident but now he didn't like the thought of her blaming herself as she would undoubtedly do.

Skye sat up and stretched like a kitten. 'I should leave.' She reached for her kicked-off shoes.

He stood up. 'I'll walk you back. Here, you wear my jacket; I'll get another one.'

As they passed through the hall his mother was saying, 'And so of course Ross and Skye immediately went to find him and . . . '

'Ross.' Skye put her hand through his arm as they walked back to the restaurant. 'Can I ask why you and Stella split up? Maddie said that she didn't know but there was no one else involved.'

'No. I mean, no, you can't ask.' Ross squeezed the arm Skye was holding, hoping that the small gesture would take away the sting of his reply. 'It's nobody else's business.' And of course it was something he'd asked himself over and over and still had not come up with an answer. Although Skye had inadvertently told him something he'd wondered about: Stella had evidently not confided in her sister.

'Well, you know where to find me,' Skye said. She released her hand as they arrived at the side door of the restaurant that led up to the flat.

'What do you mean?'

'If you ever get over her.'

'I am.'

'Yeah, 'course you are.' She took off his jacket and handed it to him. 'I won't see you in the morning. I'm getting the early bus

255

— back to the flat first and then off to my mum's.'

'Thanks for helping us out in the kitchen,' he said, 'and for your company tonight.'

'What are friends for?' said Skye.

12

The ringtone reached her through her half-awake fogginess. She'd been quite sure she wouldn't sleep a wink but she must have done.

'How're you doing in Heatherland? How's your gran?'

'Pete.' She sat up and rubbed her eyes.

'Did I wake you up?'

She held out the phone and peered at it to see the time. 'Ten o'clock! Is everything all right?'

'That's what I rang to ask you. It's a social call. On Saturday. Christmas Eve. So how is she?'

'She should get out the day after tomorrow, thank goodness, although her ankle will be in plaster for ages. I'll have to get some care sorted out for her, for after I go back to London — she'll need more help than the friend she lives with will be able to give, I think.'

'Good to hear,' Pete said, 'that she's on mend, I mean.'

'And, it's all been amazing, but she's got a brother in Australia, he was adopted and she never heard from him in seventy years but now she has. That's where my sister's gone.'

'To Coolharbour?'

'Yes, she says it's wonderful.'

'Turns out my wife's got friends of friends there — what's the brother's name?'

'Charlie, Charlie Hollis.'

'I'll pass that on. Tell me all about it when you get back.' Pete's tone changed a little. 'Nathan's set up another meeting with your man at InsideOut, ninth of January. You'll be back for that?'

So not just a social call then.

'Definitely.' She crossed her fingers. 'Back to the fray. Bye, Pete. Have a lovely Christmas.'

She leaned back against the bedhead and pulled the duvet round her against the chilly morning — and remembered, with a pang of horror, what Pete's call had temporarily put out of her mind. Gray had crashed his car after leaving her last night. He was fine, Bette assured her, shaken up a little of course. But then it transpired that Bette hadn't even seen him until much later when he was asleep so how did she know how he was really? She wasn't even sure how it had happened, only that 'Ross and Skye' had got to him as quickly as they could. Ross and Skye. The names sounded as though they should always go together like . . . like Romeo and Juliet. Victoria and Albert. Fish and chips.

Her second pang of horror came when she recalled how she'd literally wept on Gray's shoulder last night — not only did he now know Alice's secret but perhaps thinking about what she'd told him had caused him to lose concentration when he was driving. His accident was all her fault — doubly so, because he wouldn't have been in his car last night if he hadn't been doing her a kindness. If he had any repercussions from that she'd never forgive herself.

So the first thing she must do was phone to see how Gray was this morning. Then she'd have a shower and wash her hair. She'd go out — she needed to buy herself some food for tomorrow, Christmas Day. She'd get some croissants too and have them with a cafetière of coffee. And when she'd finished her late breakfast it would be time to go and see Alice and tell her the joyful news about Charlie coming to visit.

Maddie's other news would be best told by herself but Alice would be ecstatic to hear that Maddie wanted to move back home, and about her plans for the future. And she was being very practical for once. There was plenty of room in Hill View for Maddie to have workspace and the money saved from renting her room in the flat and the workshop in Edinburgh could go towards a shop unit in Melrose when a suitable one became available.

Maddie was sure to know plenty of people making beautiful things that could be stocked in the shop; there was Skye's pottery for a start. Hmm. Maybe Skye would be moving to Melrose too of course. *Ross and Skye.*

That must be Skye she could hear in the shower although she hadn't been aware of her coming in this morning. Isabel would be at work and she was catching the train to Stirling straight after she finished.

With any luck Skye would be keen to get away as well to wherever her mum lived and Stella wouldn't have to see her again.

She was astonished and delighted to hear Gray at the other end of the line when she phoned Priorsford Road.

'Lot of fuss about nothing.' He brushed aside her anxious questions. 'Bette hauled me off to the doc. I'll live. I'll see you at the hospital this afternoon.'

'You're still coming in?'

'Of course.'

'Right,' she said weakly, 'I'll see you there.'

There was a tap on her door. Skye looked round it, her hair wrapped in a towel.

'You are in. I wasn't sure,' she said. 'Any

word of Mr Ramsay this morning?'

'Gray? I spoke to him a few minutes ago — he sounded fine. Determined to come up to see Alice this afternoon.'

'I'm glad. Ross was really worried about him.'

'He would be. They're very close.'

'I've heard from Mads,' Skye said. 'She's jammy, isn't she? Christmas in the sun. And all those fit Aussies. Maybe she'll bring one back in her suitcase for me.'

'Maybe.' Skye was being friendly but Stella found it hard to be light-hearted in return. A 'fit Aussie', when she had Ross!

'I'll see you next week, then.' Skye hovered at the door as if there was something she would like to say. 'Hope Santa's good to you! Bye.'

She'd get through Christmas. She'd get Alice home. She'd get through New Year. And then she'd go back to London. A fresh start. She'd have to let Nathan down gently — she'd hardly thought about him during the last few days; that had to mean something.

There would have to be more in her life though. More than flat, tube, office, tube, flat. Perhaps she should try online dating — Jane from the office went out with a different man every week or so it seemed.

But before any of that there was something

she had to do. Unfinished business . . .

This afternoon she would take a deep breath and ask Gray for Ross's mobile number as she didn't have it any more. She would take an even deeper breath and she would ring him. Keeping her voice very steady, she would tell him she'd gone to London because Alice had incurred a large debt and she had undertaken to pay it off. She was so very sorry that she hadn't been able to tell him at the time and that if she could go back she would have tried to get round that, handle things differently somehow. She would wish him and Skye all the best. She would say goodbye in a dignified manner. And that would be the end of it.

These sound and sensible plans sat like a lead weight in the middle of her chest.

★ ★ ★

'So how did it go? We still in business?' Tom asked as he put on his whites.

'No problems at all with the cooking. Skye coped well. And the mushroom risotto went down a storm at lunchtime. We had an unexpected end to the evening though.' Ross told Tom about Gray's 'argument' with a fence post. 'Gav had the car towed back to the garage this morning.'

Tom whistled. 'But your grandpa wasn't hurt, was he?'

'Up at his usual time this morning. He swears he feels fine but he's not quite himself I don't think, and neither does Mum.'

'And your dad's back? Hey, I've only been away for twenty-four hours! It's all been happening here.' Tom put brussels sprouts, parsnips and a couple of red cabbages on the table ready for prepping.

'He is,' Ross confirmed. 'Not that I've had much chance to catch up with him yet. But when lunches are finished he's going to come along here and we'll see if we can manage a bit of a walk up the hill.' Perhaps now would be a chance to sound Tom out about the flat before his kitchen assistant arrived. 'Tom, you know that Dad's back in Scotland for good this time?'

'Aye, your mum was telling me. They're moving over Glasgow way, she said. That'll be a bit of a change for you all.'

'And maybe for you. I'll move back home with my grandpa. What would you think about taking on the flat? I'll do it up,' Ross added hastily, remembering that Tom had seen round the place when he'd helped carry the new fridge upstairs. 'It's a time-warp, I know.'

'I'm not bothered about the decor. I'm

263

retro myself.' Tom grinned. 'That would be grand, Ross, if you're sure. That landlady of mine — well, I'll be glad to see the back of her. And it'll be a relief not to have the drive every day.'

'That's settled then.'

So the die was cast there. No going back. As soon as New Year was over he'd arrange — despite Tom's comment about the wallpaper — to have the flat replumbed, rewired and decorated. One plan coming to fruition.

However, his plan to have a walk with his father didn't work out.

'Ross.' Even in that one syllable Gray sounded almost as agitated as he had last night, when he phoned Ross later in the morning.

'Grandpa? Everything all right?'

'No — we were going to the Infirmary to see Alice and of course I don't have a car now. Could you drive us?'

Drive to the hospital when there was a chance he might see Stella. He would very much rather not, but concern for Gray overrode that.

He organised a member of staff to take his place — thank goodness he had staff he could rely on — but it was a bad time to be leaving the restaurant. It was almost half-past one when he was able to get away. Gray and Bette were waiting on the doorstep, Gray looking at his watch.

'We'll be late. Visiting time's only till four.'

'We should get there before three, Grandpa.' Ross held the passenger door open for him.

'Hang on a minute.' Ross looked at his grandfather and then round at his mother in the back seat. Why can't you go in Mum's car? he was going to say, but he could hardly tell them he was backing out now. Besides, he didn't want to upset Gray who sat in uncharacteristic silence beside him.

He started the car and concentrated on the road. Fortunately, yesterday's mist had lifted and the weather was crisp and clear. Gray should still have plenty of time with Alice.

* * *

If Alice's ankle hadn't been in plaster she would have got out of bed and jumped for joy when Stella told her that she and Charlie would soon be reunited.

'I've only got one photo of him. Uncle Frank took it almost seventy years ago,' she said. 'He was a lovely little boy. I'll show you it to you when I get home.'

Stella clicked on the text Maddie had sent her with its attached picture. She enlarged it and passed the phone to Alice.

'That's what he looks like now,' she said.

Leaving Alice to pore over the photograph, she went to look out of the window. She should have told Alice as soon as she came in that she'd blurted out her secret to Gray; now she didn't want to burst her granny's bubble of happiness.

Alice had run out of paper hankies so when Gray and Bette arrived Stella would pop down to the shop. Had Gray misunderstood the visiting times? It was five to three. She thought he'd have been here sharp at 2.30 — surely he wasn't having any ill effects from his accident?

She breathed a sigh of relief. A tall figure with dandelion-clock hair could be seen striding across the car park, his daughter trying to keep up with him.

'There's Gray and Bette,' she said. 'I'll go down and meet them and get your tissues.'

Alice blew her a kiss, hardly bearing to take her eyes off her brother.

Down on the ground floor, Gray and Bette were coming through the revolving door.

'Are you all right?' She ran to hug Gray.

He didn't answer that. 'I asked Ross to drive us up,' he said in her ear. 'Please tell him what you told me yesterday.' He stepped back. 'How is Alice?'

'She's definitely on the up.' Stella smiled at Bette. 'She can have two visitors at a time so I'll just — '

'No.'

They looked at Gray in surprise.

'I will see Alice on my own first,' he said. 'Remind me where the lift is, Stella, if you would.'

Stella took him along and waited until he had pressed the button and the door closed.

'He is behaving oddly,' Bette said. 'Nothing to do with his accident, I don't think. His car's in the garage — we could have gone in mine of course but he insisted on enlisting Ross as chauffeur. And what's he up to now, marching off like that?'

Stella shrugged her shoulders helplessly. 'Is Ross coming in?' she asked.

'No, he's waiting in the car.'

She should get it over with, do what Gray said — tell Ross face-to-face what she'd been mentally rehearsing this morning. 'I'm going out to have a quick word,' she said to Bette. 'Can you point out where he's parked? I won't be long.'

Bette's eyes were full of questions but she gave her directions and 'Off you go, my dear' was all she said.

Once outside, she regretted that her jacket was upstairs in the ward — the Christmas jumper she'd worn again today offered only limited warmth out here in the car park. She tapped on his window and stood wrapping her arms around herself, although it wasn't just the cold air that was making her shiver.

Ross turned off the radio and got out. He leaned against the car, his arms folded, his eyes expressionless. Dark trousers, white shirt — he always did scrub up well.

She spoke to him with her gaze fixed over his right shoulder. 'Ross, I'll be going back to London straight after New Year, as soon as I've got Alice taken care of. I wanted to say I wish you and Skye all the best.'

No! Mentally she clapped herself on the forehead. That wasn't what she planned to say first; that was to have been her parting shot. She began again, talking as if she were reading from a script with the words she'd thought out earlier.

'Hold on, hold on.' Ross stood up straight and raised his hand. 'I don't know where to start with all this. You took the job in London to pay a debt of Alice's? Why did you do that?'

His dark blue eyes weren't expressionless now. They were bewildered.

'Because Alice brought us up. She means everything to Maddie and me.'

'I can see that of course,' he said, 'but what

I don't get is why you had to take it on and not, well, I don't know, sort something out with the bank?'

'It was nothing to do with the bank. It was a debt from a loan company. It has to be paid back as quickly as possible because the interest accumulates at a very high rate.'

'But why couldn't you tell me? I thought you . . . does Grandpa know?'

Stella rubbed her cold hands up and down her sleeves. 'No one knew until yesterday — but Gray does now. Alice told me in the afternoon that she'd borrowed from another source to pay for Maddie's fare — I asked Gray if it was him but he said it wasn't.'

'That's what that was all about.' Ross's face cleared a little. 'I thought he was confused after his crash.'

'What?'

'He asked me if I'd lent the money for the fare. I didn't, by the way.'

'Anyway, it all came out then. I'm sorry. It's hard to explain.'

'Can you try? Because I really really still don't understand.'

Why hadn't he just listened to her apology and let her walk away? She blew on her hands to try and warm them.

'Do you want to sit in the car?'

She shook her head, to indicate no, but also

to try to sort out her thoughts. This was going off-script. 'Alice and Maddie are so alike,' she said eventually. 'Even when I was only about eight I was the one who tidied up after both of them when they'd been having a craft session. I was the one who said it was time for Maddie and me to go to bed. The one who reminded Alice about lunch money and new school uniforms. The boring practical one.'

'You were too young to cope with all that.'

She didn't want his sympathy, if that's what it was. 'I didn't mind. I never thought about it until now. That's the way it was. I should have taken over the money side of things too.'

'Stella.' For a moment she thought he was going to reach out to her but that was wishful thinking. 'Alice might be dreamy and laidback but she was the grown-up, not you. You can't blame yourself for her problems.'

Isabel had said something similar. Neither of them understood — or she wasn't able to make them understand. She tried again. 'Well, I do. Especially in the few years before . . . before I found out there was a problem. I was a trained accountant for goodness' sake.'

'Yes, working hard, passing all your exams with flying colours, working your way up the firm. You were in Edinburgh, you weren't living at home. You had other things to think about — what's wrong with that? You've no

270

reason to feel guilty.'

Stella swallowed. *And falling in love with you. That occupied a lot of my time.*

Now that she'd started she would see it through if it killed her. If she didn't die of frostbite first. 'Alice has always hated talking about money; she's not materialistic and she has no head for figures at all. So she didn't read the small print in the documents she signed — she had no idea what she was getting into. She cried and cried when I found the statements; she'd stopped even opening them weeks before. It was awful, and it would have felt like a betrayal to tell anyone. So I made the decision not to, and once I'd done that it felt like there was no going back. I just put my head down and got on with it.'

'But what about me? What about us?' Ross's voice cracked.

'There was no going back,' Stella repeated. She felt her eyes brim up and blinked furiously. 'I didn't want to lie so it seemed best not to say anything. It's only now, these past few days, that I've allowed myself to think about what I did to you, running away without an explanation. I've made such a mess of everything. I'm so sorry.' She dashed her arm over her eyes. 'I hope that you can forgive me and we can part as friends.'

This was when she should put out her hand for Ross to shake but she couldn't do it.

'For God's sake, Stella. I don't want to be your friend.'

'What?' The words were like a blow.

'I want . . . is there anyone else? In London?'

'No.' Not in the way he meant. 'But now that we've cleared the air I hope I can move on, like you.' I won't cry, she told herself, I won't.

'Move on? When the last fifteen months have been . . . what do you mean 'like you'?'

'Skye, of course. She's a sweet girl.'

'You said something about Skye at the beginning of this conversation. I did — we did — '

'Ross, I know she's been in Melrose the last two nights.'

'Yes, but not in the way you're thinking.' His face flushed. 'We did get together a few months ago but it was never going to be a serious thing.'

'So you're not going out with her? But why was she — ?'

For the first time in so long Stella saw a hint of a smile on Ross's face when he looked at her. 'No, I'm not. Tom, my regular chef, was away and Skye came down to cover for him.'

'She went down to cook for you? She's not your girlfriend?'

Ross took a step towards her. 'Can we stop talking about Skye?'

And there he was, her own Ross, looking at her the way he used to, not with the indifferent mask she'd seen the last few days.

'Can we work it out?' He came closer. 'Start again? If you feel the same. I love you, Stella. I never stopped. I tried to but I couldn't do it.'

She ran into his arms. 'Oh yes. Are you sure? After the way I treated you?'

'I'm sure.' Ross found her lips with his and began to make up for the last fifteen months.

'Come and sit in the car,' he said a few minutes later, 'before you turn into an icicle.'

Reluctantly, Stella lifted her left arm from around his neck so that she could look at her watch.

'It's quarter to four!' she said. 'Your poor mum! I left her in the foyer saying I wouldn't be long. And Alice will be wondering where I am. I was supposed to be buying her tissues.'

'I don't think either of them will mind, do you? I know Mum always hoped that we'd get back together. And I think Alice will be pleased.' He put his arm around Stella as they crossed the car park.

'She'll be thrilled to bits,' Stella said. 'I

can't wait to tell her.'

Bette was nowhere in sight so they got the lift up to the ward on their own. It felt to Stella as they kissed again as if light years had passed since she'd got the lift down, unhappy and uncertain about the rest of her life.

Ross put his finger under Stella's chin and tipped up her face. 'Stay with me tonight? Or shall I take Grandpa and Mum home and come back to Maddie's flat? Whichever you want.'

Tonight. Christmas Eve.

'What about Bette's party? You should be there.'

'We should be there. But she put it off until Hogmanay because of Alice. So tonight is just for you and me and I don't think we'll be needing any mistletoe.'

To wake up with Ross on Christmas morning. Perhaps the fairy had been listening after all.

The lift stopped and the doors slid open. Bette stood there, her face alight with excitement.

'There you are! I was coming to find you, Stella.' She obviously didn't take in that they were both there, standing close together. 'You'll never guess: Gray and Alice are going to be married!'

Stella peeked round the door of the ward. Gray was sitting in the chair holding Alice's hand.

She tried to take in the news as she went over to them. She knew that Gray and Alice had been friends and neighbours for a very long time, that they were fond of each other, but she'd never dreamt that this would happen. Had they each harboured romantic feelings for the other for years and years or had Cupid mischievously bided his time before firing his arrow? But then the ways of Cupid were mysterious — she knew that better than anybody.

Gray stood up. 'Bette's told you?'

'I can't believe it. You're going to be my step-grandpa!' She flung her arms round his neck for a moment before bending over to kiss Alice. 'What a wonderful day for you.' She didn't say that it was a truly wonderful day for her as well. That could wait. This was Alice's moment.

'Oh, lovey, isn't it? I'm so lucky. I hope this silly ankle doesn't take long to heal. How can I get married with it in plaster?'

'We'll get married whenever you want, plaster or no plaster,' Gray said. 'The main thing is I'm here to look after you now.' He sat down again and patted Alice's arm but he was looking at Stella, his eyes saying, *Everything's going to be fine for you too. You don't have to do it all any more. We're in it together.*

'Oh.' Alice clasped her hands under her chin, her pansy-brown eyes shining. 'I've had a wonderful thought. Maybe we could be married when Charlie comes over — he could give me away, if that doesn't sound crazy for an old lady.'

'Less of the 'old lady'!' Stella said. Charlie would be coming over in a few weeks, Maddie had said. Not a long time in which to arrange a wedding . . . But Alice looked so happy. 'That would be perfect, wouldn't it?'

'Absolutely perfect,' said Alice.

A bell rang. The visitors at the other beds began to gather up their belongings. Gray leaned down and kissed Alice on the forehead. 'I'll hang about here and come back at half past six.'

Alice caught Stella by the hand before she could follow Gray out of the ward. 'I told Gray about you-know-what. He tried to take it as a new story but I could see in his face that he knew. He said you hadn't meant to tell him but it just came out.'

'I'm sorry,' Stella said. 'That's what

happened. But I'm glad you told him — you shouldn't have any secrets from him now.'

'I'm the one who's sorry,' said Alice. 'I should never have allowed you.'

Stella didn't want Alice to follow a train of thought that would lead to the harsh truth that the debt had been the cause of the break-up with Ross. It would be painful for both of them, and in any case that was water under the bridge now — and that was news she'd save for tomorrow. Besides, Alice was looking pale and tired — if they'd thought she was well enough surely they would have let her out for Christmas.

'Don't think about it,' she said. 'Try and sleep. We'll see you later.'

Outside in the corridor Gray had a broad smile on his face as he stood with his daughter and grandson. 'And I understand you've got some news for me, Stella?'

'Ross and I have some news for you,' Stella amended happily. 'He knows all about everything and, well, we've made up.'

'He's just told me,' Bette said. 'Thank goodness. Perhaps we'll get a smile out of him now.'

Gray clapped Ross on the back. 'Great news. Great news. Alice will be delighted.'

'Grandpa, you've got great news yourself!

So that's what you were up to.' He pulled Stella close to him. 'Love is in the air this afternoon.'

'I think we should wait until tomorrow to tell Alice about us. She's had a proposal of marriage' — Stella flashed a grin at Gray — 'and she's also seen her brother for the first time in almost seventy years. Maddie texted a photo of him. I think she's had enough excitement for one day.'

'That sounds sensible,' said Bette. 'I'd love to hear more about Alice's brother. Dad, what do you want to do? Shall we go and have a cup of tea and wait until you can go and see Alice again — if that would be all right with you, Ross?'

'Sure,' Ross said. 'I'd like to hear the Australian story too.' His arm tightened around Stella. *Have to wait a little while longer until we're alone.*

'I'm not going to tell Alice this,' Stella said, as they sat down in the café. 'Maddie can give her news — more good news! — herself. She wants to move back home, work from the house, and she says she'd like to open a shop in Melrose like one that Charlie's grand-daughter has . . . oh, but how will that work out now? With Alice and you? And what about Lilias?'

'Stella.' Ross and his grandfather spoke in

unison, evidently two minds with a single thought.

Gray wagged his finger at her. 'It will all work out, Stella, don't you fret. Let's enjoy the moment. There are undoubtedly practicalities to think about but there's nothing we can do about them today. Let's be seeing that photo of your long-lost uncle.'

Stella fished out her phone. 'Oh, no,' she said in exasperation, 'I've got a text from my boss.' She'd spoken to Pete this morning — what more was there to say? Out of force of habit she clicked to read it.

'Isn't this brilliant?' She looked up, a big smile on her face. 'Pete says that his wife asked a friend who knows someone in Coolharbour. Apparently Charlie is a very big noise there, a much-respected artist and 'an absolute gem of a man'.'

As she had done for Alice she enlarged the photograph to show them a cheerful-looking man with hazel eyes and receding silvery-fair hair. She told them the little she knew about Charlie. 'Alice is going to write it all down,' she said, 'and it will be interesting to hear from him how he found her.'

'It happened a lot then, I believe,' said Gray, 'children being adopted for economic reasons and a lot of them went abroad. Very sad. But,' he raised his teacup, 'they'll see each other soon, and today our two families have been united. Cheers!'

'Cheers!' Stella bumped her cup against his. He'd always been the grandfather figure in her life and soon the relationship would be official.

'I was thinking about tomorrow,' Bette said. 'I know that visiting hours are more flexible on Christmas Day so Kenneth could take you,' she turned to Gray, 'and Stella up around midday.'

'The restaurant's open for Christmas lunch,' Ross said apologetically to Stella. 'I'll be finished around five, I hope.'

'You'll have the afternoon with Alice and then we'll have our Christmas dinner when you get back.' Bette went on. She looked at her son, a spark of mischief in her eyes. 'Santa hats optional.'

Ross reached for Stella's hand under the table and laughed. 'I wouldn't rule them out.'

Stella could picture it now. The dining room in Priorsford Road. Glittering tree in the bay window. Delicious food and wine. Crackers. Maybe Santa hats! She recognised the reference to the romantic films she loved to watch at this time of year. It would be perfect if Alice and Maddie could be there, but everyone else she loved would be sitting round the table. Especially one person.

'Stella, how about you and Ross go now and get anything you need from Maddie's flat?' Bette suggested matter-of-factly. 'You'll be coming back to Melrose tonight?'

Stella nodded, clutching Ross's hand tightly. Yes, she would. Back where she belonged.

13

'Do you remember the first night we spent together?' Ross asked. He turned onto his side and traced his finger down Stella's face.

'What do you think? Of course. And the night I thought was going to be the last one.'

'Ssh.' He kissed her. 'No thinking about the bad times, Star. It's Christmas morning. And you're my best present ever.'

She wound her arms around his neck. 'And you're mine.' Star. It had been so long since she'd heard that name.

'I wish I didn't have to leave you,' Ross said, 'but Tom and the rest of the staff will be here soon. What'll you do until it's time to go and see Alice? I'm sorry this place is so grotty. Not somewhere you'd want to spend any time.'

Stella looked around. 'I suppose it is. I never noticed last night. Other things on my mind.' She smiled at him. 'I thought I'd see Lilias before I go round to Priorsford Road.'

'Lilias!' Ross groaned. 'The range. We'll go to Hill View together, shall we?' Reluctantly, he pushed the duvet aside. 'What would I

282

give to stay right here and not see anyone else today?'

As he headed for the shower Stella curled up happily — or as happily as she could on the rather lumpy mattress. This time yesterday she'd been rehearsing the Goodbye Ross speech she would make, and thinking of the future with dismay. Now she felt as if all her Christmases had come at once.

★　★　★

Lilias was nowhere to be seen when Stella knocked at the back door, and called 'Happy Christmas, Lilias!' Leaving Ross to fire up the range she checked the other rooms on the ground floor before going upstairs. Lilias was in a room at the front, paintbrush in hand. The furniture had been pushed back to stand round the walls, leaving only an easel in the middle of the carpet.

'This is for Ross,' Lilias said. 'I thought of it in the middle of the night so I got up right then and started it.'

Stella went closer to the easel. Greens, brown, purple, in the style of the seascape in the Edinburgh gallery, and the picture of the house Lilias had done for Alice — whose hanging had caused Alice to fall and Stella to come home. So really it was, in a roundabout way, thanks to Lilias that she and Ross were back together. Impulsively, Stella hugged her.

Lilias took the endearment as a comment on the painting. 'I know he loves the hills,' she said. Then she stopped being the competent artist and reverted to the dithery side of her. 'Gray and Bette came in yesterday evening. How wonderful! They said that Alice should be home tomorrow. But what should I do, Stella dear? She won't be able to climb the stairs . . . downstairs bedroom . . . fresh sheets . . . but that washing machine, all the dials, I don't know — '

'I'll sort it out. That's a very good idea,' Stella said. 'Did they tell you that Gray and I will be spending the afternoon with Alice? Kenneth's driving — would you like to come? Alice would love to see you.'

Lilias shrank back. 'Oh no, dear. That smell. The doctors. I don't want to go. Do I have to?'

Poor Lilias. Stella hadn't expected that reaction. 'Of course not. That's fine, don't worry. You'll see her tomorrow. You carry on painting and I'll organise the downstairs bedroom for Alice.'

Downstairs the range was beginning to glow.

'I'll see you later,' Ross said. He held out his arms. 'I still can't believe you're here.'

'We have a lot of time to make up.' And a lot of talking to do, she thought, about how a long-distance relationship was going to work, but for the moment actions spoke louder than words.

* * *

All this lovely information was bursting to be told and she couldn't share half of it, Stella thought as she went to tell Lilias she was going. She knocked on the door — maybe Lilias wouldn't like to be interrupted. But she wasn't painting; she was gazing out of the window, paintbrush in hand, recalling perhaps how that view looked in late summer before transferring it to the canvas.

It should really be Alice who should tell Lilias about her own forthcoming change in circumstance, but Stella would leave it to Gray to break the news later this evening. And she didn't want to talk about herself and Ross before she'd even told Alice and Maddie — although if Lilias had been downstairs earlier she would have seen them arrive together. But she could tell her now about Charlie and about how he and Alice would shortly be reunited.

'I remember when Alice opened his letter,' Lilias said. 'She went so pale I thought she would faint. I made her some camomile tea and she told me all about it, about her daddy being injured in the war and coming home one day to find her brother gone. 'I wish I could go straight out there to see him, Lilias,' she said, 'but it's so far away I don't know if I'd manage, and of course it would cost such a lot.' That's when I had my idea.'

Stella stared at her. 'It was your idea about Maddie?'

'I said to Alice, 'Why not ask Maddie to go?'' Lilias nodded. 'I said I'd buy her ticket. Of course there's not a travel agent in Melrose, and I've never bought anything on that web, but I meant I would pay for it.'

'You lent Alice the money for the ticket? That was very good of you, Lilias. I did wonder how — '

'We had a little argument about it, Alice and I. I wanted to give her the money but she would only take it as a loan.'

'It's a lot to give,' Stella said. 'We must pay you back.'

Lilias shook her head. 'I owe Alice much more than money, Stella dear. She asked me to come here when I didn't want to live on my own. And she had a man come to look at my paintings. He sent me a big cheque for them.'

Well, no doubt the argument would

continue, but it was a weight off Stella's mind to know that it was Lilias — kept it in the family so to speak. It was true that she'd been living with Alice all these months and it was entirely thanks to Alice's efforts that she was having a swansong with her work.

'I saw one of your paintings in a gallery window in Edinburgh the other day,' she said. She wondered if it now hung in the well-heeled couple's house. Lucky them. 'It was beautiful.'

'Yes, the gallery man. All thanks to Alice.'

'So I'm off now but I'll see you later, at Gray's, for Christmas dinner. I'll call for you, shall I? About six?'

Lilias paused, her eyes suddenly shrewd. 'You'll be there, Stella dear? At Gray's house?'

There wasn't any way Lilias could tell Alice before Stella herself did. 'Er, yes. Ross and I, we're . . . we're friends again.'

Lilias waved the paintbrush around in excitement. A blob of purple paint landed on Stella's jumper — the silvery-green starry Christmas jumper being worn for the third day in a row, but hey, today was Christmas Day!

'I'm so sorry, Stella dear.' Lilias fluttered towards her with a palette knife and a bottle of turpentine. 'Let me — I'm so glad — will you move back home?'

Stella concentrated on removing the paint. Great. Now she was going to smell of turps. When she looked up again Lilias had moved back to the easel, her question forgotten.

★ ★ ★

It was only five days since she'd visited the house in Priorsford Road but it might have been another lifetime, it seemed so long ago. Stella rang the bell and as she waited she stood back to look at the house that had been Gray's home for decades, and her second home when she was growing up.

It was a traditional Scottish Victorian house, its stone mellowed with age. There were bay windows on either side of the door, one with a Christmas tree in it, and three windows above. They were framed by a spider's web of branches at this time of year — in the summer the walls were glorious with red Virginia creeper.

'My dear, you don't need to ring the bell. Happy Christmas! Come in.' Bette, not usually demonstrative, gave Stella a warm hug. 'I knew there must have been some misunderstanding and I don't want to know the details; I'm only glad it's all cleared up.

There's no one I'd rather see with Ross than you.'

Stella hugged her back. 'It's been horrible,' she said. 'I'm sorry that — '

Bette hugged her again before letting her go. 'No, don't say any more. It's all behind us. It's the future that matters. Come and have a cup of coffee.'

On the kitchen table there were several cardboard boxes. Bette pushed them to one end.

'I'm making a start on sorting out what's ours and what's Dad's. It's not easy — do you know it's seventeen years since we moved in here with him?'

Seventeen years since she met Ross then. 'When are you leaving?'

'In a couple of months. We've had an offer accepted on a house in Rutherglen but the sellers can't get into their new home until the end of February. Look, this box has photographs.' She fished one out. 'Dad took this the first summer we were here.'

In the photo Ross was standing in between Stella and Maddie in the garden of Hill View, Maddie holding on to a big black dog.

'That must be Patch's predecessor,' Stella said.

'Goodness, that was a long time ago.' Gray had come in and he peered over Stella's shoulder. 'Happy Christmas, soon-to-be-step-granddaughter!'

'Happy Christmas! And it is, the happiest happy Christmas. And guess what?' Stella glanced at Bette. 'Long story, Bette, but, Gray, I found out this morning that it was Lilias who paid for Maddie's trip.'

Gray whistled. 'That explains that. Is she coming with us today?'

Stella shook her head. 'No. She doesn't like hospitals, I gather. But she's fine. She's begun another painting, for Ross — been up half the night working on it.'

'It's going to be an interesting household to live in,' Gray chuckled. 'Now, Bette says she'll go over to Hill View tomorrow with a casserole. All Lilias will have to do is heat it up when we get back.'

'Gray, about tomorrow, would you mind if Ross and I went to take Alice home? I don't think there's any way I can get through today without telling her that we've made up, but I'd like her to see us together, just the two of us.'

'It's a pity he can't come with us today. Of course, my lass. And I'll be waiting on the doorstep at Hill View for her.'

★   ★   ★

Bette ushered Gray and Kenneth and Stella and Lilias through to the sitting room.

'Ooh, you look lovely, Stella. Ross is in the kitchen organising drinks,' she said.

'Hey.' Ross put down the bottle of prosecco he'd taken out of the fridge and came over to kiss her. 'You're wearing that dress.'

Stella had asked Kenneth to stop at Hill View, saying she would get changed and then walk round with Lilias. She fished the red dress out of the back of the wardrobe where she'd thrust it two days ago — luckily it was made of a jersey material so it wasn't crumpled. And she'd managed to find the snowball earrings, wondering if Ross would remember what she'd been wearing that night. It seemed he had.

'I missed you,' he said. 'How was today?'

'Believe it or not, it was very merry,' Stella said. And it had been. There was Christmas music playing in the ward; the patients got a little present; the nurses sat and chatted; chocolates and sweets were passed round; and the four lots of visitors ended up talking to each other. 'Quite a party atmosphere. And the patients will be getting turkey and all the trimmings for dinner.'

Talking of turkey, she was suddenly aware of all the delicious smells that were in this kitchen; the turkey was on a board ready for carving and there were numerous pots and pans on top of the cooker. 'I must ask Bette if there's anything I can do to help.'

Ross held on to her. 'What did Alice say? About us?'

'She cried.'

'Oh no! I thought she'd be pleased.'

'Duh.' Stella stood on tiptoe to bump her head against his. 'Cried with joy. Really — she's been fretting over it so much.'

'What time do we pick her up tomorrow?'

'They said about half past two. When will you get away?'

'The shop won't be open until the day after. And we're only doing restaurant lunches again, not dinner. What's the point of being the boss if you can't delegate? I have delegated and I am at your disposal all day. Do with me what you will.'

'Ooh, brilliant.' She thought of the sights she'd stood and looked at on Thursday — how much more fun it would be to see them with Ross. 'How about going into Edinburgh in the morning? Alice and Maddie and I loved going up in the wheel last year' — not that she wanted to think about last Christmas but somehow doing all the same Christmassy things with him this year would cancel out how miserable she'd felt then — 'and there's loads of other things going on.'

'And lunch? I'll do some research, book somewhere nice.'

'Who's talking about lunch?' Bette came in. 'Let's have dinner! Stella dear, under that cloth there's a platter of smoked salmon blinis if you'd like to take it through. You've got the fizz, Ross? I've put the glasses out. Your grandpa wants to make a toast.'

Or several toasts as it turned out. To absent friends, meaning Alice and Maddie of course. To Ross and Stella being reunited. To Kenneth's return. To Lilias, who went pink-cheeked and giggly. And to Bette for the excellent dinner they were about to have.

'And to you,' Ross and Stella said to him at the same time.

Ross's grandfather. Stella's soon-to-be-step-grandfather. It was amazing the way life took unexpected twists and turns.

★   ★   ★

'Somewhere nice' was on the third floor of an eatery just below Edinburgh Castle, with a view over the city and lovely food. Far below them were the wheel and the other Christmas attractions they'd spent an enjoyable two hours exploring.

Ross raised his hand for the bill. 'Shall we have a walk up to the castle? For old times' sake? We've got enough time.'

So he was remembering that day too.

The weather had changed while they'd been eating. A flurry of snowflakes blew in their faces as they made their way on to the castle ramparts, feeling the chill after the heat of the restaurant.

'Maybe a very short walk,' Ross amended, rubbing his hands together. He measured the length of the wall with his eye. 'About here, was it? Would they let us put up a plaque, do you think?'

'Saying, *It was on this spot in March 2015 that Ross Drummond and Stella Greenlaw first declared their love*,' Stella said. 'Although I'm not sure this is the spot actually; I think it was nearer the castle.'

'Was it? We'll have to get it right. Perhaps we should do the declaring again.'

'We should. Definitely. Can we have two plaques then?'

'All the way along, dozens of them.' With both hands Ross lifted Stella's windswept hair away from her face. 'I love you, Star.'

'I love you.'

Their cold lips met, became warm.

'Ross.' Stella clung to him. Maybe it would spoil the moment but she had to say it. 'You know I must go back to London after New Year? I can't move home. Not yet.' Alice marrying Gray made no difference to the fact that the debt had to be paid off and she was the one to do it, see through what she'd started. But she had even more incentive now to work hard, to learn all she could, so that she could be promoted . . . back to the Edinburgh office.

He held her tighter. 'I know. But this time it will be different. I'll come down as often as I can, or we can meet halfway. And we can text and phone and Skype. Shout very loudly.'

'I love you.'

'I love you too. Three plaques. Do you want to go for a fourth one or leave it for another day?'

'We'll be back. I think we'll have to make a move now — you look like Frosty the Snowman.' Snowflakes dusted his eyelashes and his hair, and her own face felt icy cold.

Hand in hand they ran as safely as they could down the steps and along the road to the car park on Castle Terrace.

'Look,' he said, shutting the car door and reaching behind him. 'I brought a travelling rug for Alice but you put it over yourself for now. The car will soon heat up.'

'Thank you — that was really thoughtful. Alice will be so happy to be coming home.'

'And her *fiancé* will be waiting on the

doorstep for her.' Ross grinned. 'Can you believe it?'

'I guess it will be a small affair but I don't know how this wedding is going to be arranged in time for Charlie coming over,' Stella said. 'I can only do so much from down south.'

'Are you kidding? Mum will be on the case already,' Ross said. 'And I believe there is a rather good restaurant in Melrose. Available for christening parties, weddings, etc.'

'I had heard that,' she said, pinching his arm. 'I must try it sometime.'

'What do you think will happen?' Ross asked. 'I mean, Hill View. Priorsford Road. I wonder if Grandpa has thought through the 'practicalities' as he called them.'

'I'm sure he has. He'll tell us in his own good time.'

★ ★ ★

'Stella.' Ross beckoned her to come through to the front hall in Hill View.

Gray had gone home and Alice and Lilias were talking nineteen-to-the-dozen, going over every little detail of the last few days for the umpteenth time. Soon it would be time for Stella to help Alice get ready for bed.

'What is it?'

'What we were talking about earlier in the car? Grandpa and Alice have decided that he'll move in here.'

'Really? Did he tell you?'

Ross nodded. 'When you were in the kitchen.'

'Yesterday morning,' Stella remembered, 'I was talking about Lilias and her middle-of-the-night painting session and he said something like, it will be an interesting household to live in.'

'Mum was worried about him being lonely — not much chance of that now! Three women to look after, and to look after him. He'll be in his element,' Ross said. 'But there's something else.' He took her hand. 'He's making his house over to me.'

'What?'

'It's a big house for one person. I hope it won't be too long before someone shares it with me.'

'I hope so too — at least you are referring to me, aren't you?' Stella laughed and put his hand to her lips. 'How wonderful. I've always loved that house.'

She looked around the hall, scene of the accident that had set off a long chain of events. There was something not quite right though. She led him over to the Christmas tree. 'Wait there,' she said.

'Tada!' She switched on the Christmas lights and came over to join him in front of the tree. She put her arm around his waist. 'I know it's kind of daft,' she said, 'but do you remember when we were kids, Alice got us to ask the Christmas fairy to grant a secret wish?'

'I do. And it's not so daft.' He grinned down at her. 'I wished on her once when no one was looking — to play for Scotland.'

'See!' Stella smiled back. 'It does work.'

'Did you make a wish this year?' he asked.

'It's supposed to be a secret, remember?' *I wish that Ross still loved me and we were happy again.* She reached up to kiss him. 'But I can tell you this — it's come true.'

Other titles published by Ulverscroft:

THE DRESS

Jane L. Rosen

Natalie is a Bloomingdale's salesgirl, mooning over her lawyer ex-boyfriend. Felicia has been quietly in love with her happily-married boss for twenty years; now that he's a lonely widower, the time may just be right for her to make her move. Andrea is a private detective, specializing in gathering evidence on cheating husbands, and can't figure out why her intuition tells her the guy she's tailing is one of the good ones . . . Three people leading disparate existences — yet they have more in common than they realize. For their lives — and six more — are all linked together by one little black dress . . .